Raven's Mountain

WENDY ORR

Raven's Mountain

ALLEN&UNWIN

First published in 2010

Allen & Unwin
83 Alexander Street
Crows Nest NSW 2065
Australia
Phone: (61 2) 8425 0100
Fax: (61 2) 9906 2218
Email: info@allenandunwin.com
Web: www.allenandunwin.com

A Cataloguing-in-Publication entry is available from the
National Library of Australia www.trove.nla.gov.au

ISBN 978 1 74237 465 9

Cover and text design by Ruth Grüner
Cover photo by Getty Images
Photo of Mt Rundle by Elizabeth Burridge
Set in 11.3 pt Caslon 540 by Ruth Grüner
Printed in Australia in May 2013 at McPherson's Printing Group,
76 Nelson St, Maryborough, Victoria 3465, Australia.
www.mcphersonsprinting.com.au

3 5 7 9 10 8 6 4 2

To Kathy,
because sisters are forever

W.O.

Prologue

'You'll love the mountains,' Mum says.

For one sweet hold-my-breath minute, when Mum said they had a surprise for us, I thought they meant something good, like a puppy, or a horse.

They meant they've bought a house in Jenkins Creek, where Scott grew up. We're moving. Leaving Cottonwood Bluffs and driving right across the country, over the mountains to the other side.

I've never even heard of Jenkins Creek.

'No one's heard of Jenkins Creek,' snarls Lily.

Mum and Scott are both talking at once, about every good thing they can possibly think of. An avalanche of words thuds over us: house of our own, camping and hiking, new start for our brand new family.

All I hear is that I'm leaving where I've lived my whole

life. I'm leaving Gram, Jess, Amelia and everyone else I know. Leaving the gentle flatlands of Cottonwood Bluffs. Leaving the only place my real dad might ever come back to look for us.

It feels like stepping off a footpath onto ice. The world is skidding out from under me.

1

THURSDAY AFTERNOON

The service station has bear paw prints running up the wall to the roof. I know they're just painted, but they give me the creeps. I can't help looking to see if there really is a bear up there.

But it feels good to get out of the truck and stretch. We've been on the highway for two hours – and really we've been driving for three days because we left Cottonwood Bluffs early Monday morning and only got to Jenkins Creek yesterday afternoon.

The moving van unloaded the beds and boxes and everything, and we slept in our new house last night. So today Lily and I should have started at our brand new schools where we don't know one single person – my first day of being the ginger new kid.

But Mum said that since we'd already missed the

3

first day of term, another couple wouldn't matter. Partly because Scott's bursting to show off his favourite mountains, and partly because this trip will take three days and we'd have to wait till next summer if we didn't do it now. By the next long weekend it'll be too cold. But mostly because they think that Lily and I will be happy about moving here once we stand on top of a mountain.

So now we're on the way to the great family adventure. Except that all the way up the highway, Scott's been worrying that his special campsite might have been turned into something so fancy it won't be much of an adventure.

And Mum isn't with us, so we're not actually a family. The Coffee Corner called and asked her to come in today because one of the waitresses was sick, and she said she couldn't say no to her new boss before she'd even started.

Maybe she thought climbing a mountain would be harder than Scott said.

Scott fills the truck, and buys some chewing gum because our ears are popping. We're still about half an hour from the lake, and the mountains are getting higher.

'Anything else you want, you better get it now,' he says. 'I don't know what's going to be there.'

What I want is to be home with Jess and Amelia. If I had a phone I'd send them a message: *Help! At the end of civilization! About to be eaten by bears!*

I'm not stupid enough to ask Lily to borrow hers – even if she wasn't sending her friends today's one-millionth text: *middle seat sux.* She wants me to see it so I'll feel bad, but it's not my fault we couldn't swap for two hours. I didn't even like the window seat much. People say mountains are pretty, but that's when they're on a postcard. Up close they lean over you like bullies in the playground. After a while I'd taken my glasses off so the shapes were softer and blurred.

The road we've turned onto isn't sealed, and it's even steeper and windier than Scott said. It's got a cliff on one side and nothing on the other. There's a creek a long way down at the bottom of the nothing.

I'm not crazy about the Beware of Falling Rocks signs either.

Nor is Lily. 'Great! If we don't get smashed falling *off* the rocks, we'll get crushed by rocks falling on top of us.'

'It's more about watching out for a heap on the road,' says Scott. 'You'd be unlucky to get hit by one falling that instant.'

'That's supposed to make me feel better?'

'Yup!' says Scott.

The road flattens out and twists away from the creek. Scott gets excited about a faded sign of a galloping pinto at the end of a long driveway. 'That was my buddy's grandparents' ranch!'

I can't see any horses now. Scott thinks the ranch was sold to developers after the grandparents died.

And then the road ends. There's still no sign for a resort.

Scott keeps on going, down an almost-disappeared track through the forest. Long grass swishes at the doors and branches tickle the windows. The truck jolts and thumps. Lily glares when I bump her.

A raven flaps across the track, so low and close to the windscreen it makes us all jump.

'You're thinking that's just an ordinary old raven,' Scott whispers, 'but that's Raven, the old trickster who created the world . . . and he's thinking, *Here's one of my people!*'

Lily rolls her eyes so hard I think they're going to fall out. I can't see what she's typing this time, but I can guess.

There's no reception; her message won't send.

'Nobody told me we were going into the wilderness!' she snarls.

'That's the general idea,' says Scott. He's cheered up now it doesn't look like we're heading towards a resort.

Mum says she named me after a bird because when she was pregnant, I turned and somersaulted so much it felt like wings tickling her insides.

So she called me Raven.

But it was my dad who flew away.

There's no resort. No campground. Nothing. Not even a toilet. Just a lake with mountains all around it, layers and layers of them, every way you turn. Ours is the biggest. Right up under the clouds there's a knobby peak with a slit of mouth under a big hooked nose, and snowy eyebrows and hair. If mountains have faces, this isn't a friendly one.

'Are we really going to climb that?'

'Sure are,' says Scott.

The only thing that's changed since Scott's olden days is a giant rock wall sprawling across the grass and up through the forest. It looks like the mountain burst open, popping off trees like buttons and spilling its guts.

'Could be why there's no resort,' says Scott.

'So it's not safe to stay here!' Lily says.

'Look at the grass and moss around it – that rockfall happened years ago. The mountain's not lying in wait for us so it can do it again!'

2

When I was little, Lily was my hero. On my very first day of school she knocked down the big boy who kept rapping me on the head and calling me a redheaded woodpecker. Some nights she'd climb into bed with me and tell me stories. But ever since she turned thirteen, my sister has been Queen of the Putdown. She doesn't have to say anything: just rolls her eyes, sniffs, and looks away . . . and I realise I'm the stupidest, most immature being on earth.

Amelia thinks she's been possessed by aliens, but Jess says we should make our own pact: We won't be mean when we turn thirteen.

The air is fresh and piney. The breeze blows tiny rippling waves across the lake, and cools the backs of my sweat-sticky legs. I want to run through the long grass to the lake and splash.

But Scott says no one's running anywhere till we've learned how to use the bear spray. 'Just like Lily said, we're in the wilderness. You've got to be prepared for anything. So this goes on your belt, not inside your pack. If you need it, you'll need it fast.'

It looks like fly spray, but you can't just spray it around your tent to keep bears away – you have to wait till one's charging before you spray it in the face.

'No way am I getting close enough to a bear to spray it!' Lily exclaims.

'I'd run!'

'You can't outrun a bear!' Scott snaps, and gives us the bear lecture again, plus the cougar one. He shows us the safety catch and makes us practise using the spray, as much as you can without actually letting it off.

Lily says that because Scott has never had kids before, he has to try extra hard to be a good parent and warn us about every possible thing that could ever go wrong in every possible universe. There's no way we'd be on this mountain if he and Mum really thought we could get eaten by a bear.

Part of the fun of camping out is fishing for our dinner.

That's what Scott claims. I tell him I don't like fish.

'You would if you caught it yourself!'

He shows us how to control the line with our left hands and cast with the right. I don't exactly want to catch a fish, but I can't wait to see Scott and Lily's faces when I pull one in my first go.

First I tangle the line on a log; next I nearly wrap it around Scott's neck, and the third time the hook flies back into the toe of my sneaker.

Scott doesn't argue when I say I'm done with fishing for now.

Lily's standing on a rock with the sun setting behind her. The light's so bright that she looks shadowy; tall and mysterious, with a kind of golden halo around her. Her fishing line arcs smoothly into the lake.

After about five minutes she gets bored and sits down to paint her toenails. If she'd stayed there one more minute the fish probably would have jumped right onto her hook the way they were supposed to.

I start picking up sticks at the edge of the woods. Lily helps build a fire on the gravelly beach when her nail polish is dry.

'Look!'

A silver trout is dancing on the end of Scott's line;

it would be beautiful if it weren't fighting for its life. Scott takes it a long way around the lake to kill and clean it, so there's no smell for bears to follow. Lily and I are glad because we don't want to watch.

'I could never do that,' I say. For once, Lily agrees with me.

We light the fire and wrap the fish in foil, and the potatoes and corn on the cob we've brought from home. When the flames die down but the rocks are hot, we put the potatoes, then the corn and then the fish, into the ashes to cook.

The potatoes are crunchy and the corn's a bit black, but the fish is crispy and doesn't look anything like a fish swimming in a lake. Turns out I was hungrier than I thought.

At bedtime we drag our sleeping bags out of the tents, Lily and I on one side of the fire and Scott on the other. The ground is lumpy, frogs are croaking and mosquitoes whining, but we're too smeared with Insect-Off for them to touch us. After a while it starts to sound like a weird kind of music. When I take my glasses off the stars go blurry bright, and the Milky Way is so solid and near I feel like I could swim in it. I keep thinking: 'I'm sleeping under the stars!'

The sky and lake are still end-of-the-night grey when I wake up. Then the first edge of the sun starts creeping over the mountains, and suddenly the sky and lake are early-morning blue, and I still didn't catch the exact minute when the night turned into day.

Scott's already up; the fire's glowing and flapjacks are sizzling. I've got a feeling today isn't going to be just a good day, it's going to be one of those days – like the first time I ever rode a horse – that's like a picture framed with light. I know I'll remember it for the rest of my life.

Finally we've packed, tidied and locked the last bit of stuff into the truck. The hike can officially start. My watch says 8:25 am.

'Wouldn't it be easier to call it 7:25 like the rest of us?' Scott asks. 'You can't stay on Cottonwood Bluffs time forever!'

But if I change my watch I'll know I don't live there anymore.

The forest is all around us, thick, dark and cool. It's the same heavy quiet feeling as Gram's living room, as if you're not really supposed to be there.

I concentrate on stepping one foot in front of the other, silently as a native hunter. It's not easy when you're climbing over logs. A branch slaps my face. 'Ow! Sorry.'

'It's not a library,' Scott says. 'You're allowed to talk.'

'But that'll scare the animals!'

'That's what we want to do!' says Lily. 'It's not like we're hunting.'

'We just don't want to surprise them. If you're not hunting, you don't want to be hunted.'

'Do you ever go hunting?'

'Not anymore.'

'How come?'

'Because when I killed a bear I finally got it. One minute he was a happy, healthy animal moseying along, minding his own business, and the next he was gone – all because of me.'

There's a deer grazing just below us. My first real, live, wild animal.

Lily reaches for her camera. With one leap, the deer disappears.

Two seconds later a smaller deer bounds past us.

'Her teenage daughter,' says Scott.

Lily and I get the giggles. But I keep wondering

how the daughter deer is ever going to find her mother in that thick dark forest.

We open our packs of almonds and raisins on top of a rocky cliff. It's warm out in the sun; I wish we didn't have to go back into the trees. There's just as many of them above us as below; you can't even tell where we've been except for a splash of turquoise, way down at the bottom, that must be the lake.

I still don't see how we can climb all the way to the top and down again in one day.

Scott points down at a valley on the other side. 'Remember I showed you my buddy Greg's ranch? We used to ride all through those hills.'

'Could we have a horse now we live in the country?' Lily interrupts.

'You'd have to ask your mum.'

When Lily and I argued about moving, Mum came up with all sorts of excuses – but even when I cried she never said, 'We could have our own horse.'

'You could get one,' I suggest to Scott. 'And we could ride it.'

'Like I said, it's up to your mum.'

I didn't really think it would work. But Lily grins at me – it was worth a try.

Scott's given me the compass because I got that Girl Scout badge. The trail zigzags, but the top of the mountain is due south from the lake; I line the needle up while we're out in the open.

Except now he's got the map out because he wants to detour east to show us the most special thing in his special place. 'I promise it's worth it.'

It better be. You'd think going across would mean the ground was flatter, but mountains don't work like that; it's still hills going up and down, and the woods are nearly as thick as they were at the start.

But there's a rumbly kind of highway noise, up here where no highway can be. Luckily I realise that before I say it.

Louder and louder; the noise is like thunder. I never knew a waterfall would be so loud. It crashes over a cliff in a solid white wall of water. A pool at the bottom swirls and bubbles like Amelia's mum's hot tub.

'Take a picture for your mum,' Scott asks Lily.

'She should have come with us like she said!' Lily says, but she takes a picture anyway. She wants to send it to her friends.

We squat on the fat rocks to catch the water in our filter bottles. The spray splashes over us, as if someone's turned a sprinkler on. It's so hot it feels good.

'You think this is special?' Scott says. 'You ain't seen

nothing yet!' He scrambles halfway up the cliff beside the waterfall – and disappears. 'Come on!' His voice is like an echo from behind the thunder.

Lily shrugs.

I follow.

The cliff rocks are big, and the ones closer to the edge are wet and slippery. Falling off would hurt. I'm half scared, half not wanting to be chicken, and mostly wanting to see what's so great.

I get to the *Open Sesame!* boulder where Scott disappeared. I still can't see where he's gone.

'Slide down to the ledge!'

It's actually quite easy once you see it. I slip down and sidle along to where Scott's standing in a cave behind the waterfall.

It's funny because from the outside I couldn't see in at all. Now I'm dry and secret inside the cave, looking out at ghost trees and rainbows on the other side of the silver water.

'Magic?' asks Scott.

'Magic,' I say.

Lily won't come up. Lily hates caves.

More trees, more forest, more wondering if we'll ever get to the top of the mountain . . . Finally we're out in the sun again, in a field of orange and red berries.

At the bottom of the field is a bear.

It's just standing there, big and bearlike, munching up branches of berries, exactly like you see in pictures. Except it's white.

There's no such thing as a white bear in these mountains.

A black cub leaps at the berries bobbling from its mother's mouth. A white cub jumps on top of the black one and wrestles him to the ground. But Mama Bear's not worrying about naughty cubs: she stands up on her hind legs, tall as Scott, and sees us.

She woofs and shoos the cubs up the nearest tree – and Scott shoos Lily and me up the trail.

'Don't run,' he murmurs. 'Just keep walking.'

I look back. He's walking sideways so he's not turning his back on the bear. His can of bear spray is out of its holster and in his hand. He wants us to be afraid, so we'll pay attention to his lectures.

But around the next bend, he decides we'll be safe spying from behind a shield of rocks. He and Lily peek over the top. I find a perfect peephole at the bottom. My hands and knees are cold on the hard ground, but the rock is warm against my face.

Mama Bear's still watching and sniffing; the cubs are still up the tree, the black one at the top. A mother and two cubs: just like our family. Lily's the pretty white one that looks like her mother, and I'm the ordinary black one.

Except bear families don't have stepdads – even their own fathers sometimes eat the cubs. At least our real dad didn't try to eat me before he disappeared.

I used to make up lots of different stories about my father. When dancers from the Crow Nation came to the school, I decided that Mum had named me Raven because my real dad was Crow. Other times I thought he was a Viking, or a superhero or a cowboy.

Now I'm older I know that's not true.

My real dad lives in Australia.

He's suntanned and blond like Lily. He wears khaki shorts and shirts, says 'Crikey!' and can wrestle crocodiles and snakes, just like the Crocodile Hunter.

'Are they polar bears?' I whisper.

Lily rolls her eyes. 'Right. And we're sitting on an ice floe.'

Scott ignores her. 'The dad was probably a plain old black bear – but the mum and white cub look like Kermodes, the Spirit Bears from the coast up north.

There are lots of legends about them, like they'll dive to the bottom of lakes to get fish for people who are starving.'

Mama Bear tears off another branch of berries.

'Look, Raven: she's picking us some!'

Scott's afraid I'll believe Lily, and gives us a lecture about really they're black bears except for being white. 'It doesn't matter how pretty she is – that bear could attack if we surprised her, or she thought we were threatening her cubs, or even if she was very hungry. That's why we stick together.'

Scott and Lily pick up their packs, but I go on watching. Through the raggedy frame of my spy hole, the bears look like a scene from a fairy tale: Hansel and Gretel hiding from the witch. Hansel is the black cub and Gretel white.

Gretel nudges her brother's bottom. He slides down to her branch and shoves back. They wrestle round the branches and down the tree, swinging, clinging, sliding . . . Hansel crashes to the ground.

A raven caws, laughing.

The black cub rolls to his feet, looking around to see if anyone's watching. You can almost hear him: 'I meant to do that anyway!'

I don't tell Scott and Lily. It's a secret between the raven, the bears and me.

3

I always thought the tree line was like a border: one minute you're in the woods, and the next step you're on a bare mountain where it's too high and cold for trees to live. For some reason I thought it would be exciting. I think Lily did too; at least she didn't argue when I said we should have our lunch right on the tree line. I thought we could sit on the rocks with our feet in the forest.

It's not like that at all. It's not even a line: the trees have just been getting smaller, scrawnier and further apart, and now there are hardly any at all. Finally I choose what looks like the last sad, bent little fir and we have our lunch there.

I wonder if the tree feels like a winner or just wishes it lived a little ways down the mountain with its friends.

It feels more like mountain climbing now, because all we can see is mountains, and the one we're on is mostly rock. The only plants are tiny little bushes pushing out between the stones. And the air's getting colder, as if we're hiking towards the arctic.

We've seen six mountain goats, and Lily saw a marmot. I think I saw the raven again but I don't say anything. I don't need to hear any more legends about Raven tricking and stealing.

I'm still wishing Mum could have called me after a bird that ate something nicer than roadkill, when somebody pelts me with a handful of gravel.

Lily shrieks and runs; Scott grabs my hand and tows me towards a big overhanging rock.

Of course it's not gravel and nobody's throwing it, unless it's some cold-breathed mountain spirit. Just a hailstorm, but it's creepy the way it was sunny one minute and the next we've got hailstones as big as grapes hitting us in the face.

We dive under the rock. There's just enough room for the three of us to squat and take turns taking off our packs and pulling on our jackets.

The side of the rock's covered with lichen like tiny golden cups. I say I'm going take a patch home with some mosses from further down, to make a terrarium. Terrariums are like ant farms with no ants. Gram has one in an old fish tank with a glass lid; the plants grow and breathe and make mist that waters them so they can grow and breathe more . . .

Scott says no, because you can't pick plants in a national park, not even little ones like lichens.

I tell him it's for Mum's birthday, and he says that's a very nice idea, but it's still a national park.

Lily thinks you can tell Scott hasn't been a parent before, because he hasn't been practising saying No for as long as Mum has. I think he's starting to get the hang of it.

The hailstorm only lasts a few minutes. Maybe the mountain spirit has a mum who's told him to leave the little kids alone. We crawl out from under our rock as the sun comes out, sparkling the hailstones like diamonds.

I grab a handful and let them roll around on my tongue, ice straight from the sky.

Up ahead we can see patches of snow in dips and shadows. We're getting closer to the peak.

'Well, duh!' says Lily. 'Since we've been walking all day.'

Sometimes I don't know why I have a sister.

There's just this one bare slope to get across, and we'll be at the bottom of the knobby head.

From here the nose is more like an eagle's beak; the mouth is a crooked slit. I imagine the squinty eyes glaring, too deep for us to see, under the snow on the eyebrow ridge.

'It's just erosion,' says Scott. 'It's taken thousands of summers of melting snow to whittle out that nose. Another thousand years and it'll be gone.'

I still think it looks evil, but I don't care. I just want to climb it.

Suddenly there's a horrible gasping, wheezing noise. It sounds like when Amelia has an asthma attack. It's Lily. She's doubled over as if she can't breathe.

When Amelia sounds like that she has to have her puffer *fast*. If it was her wheezing like this she might die because we don't have a puffer and we'd have to carry her all the way down the mountain before we could take her to a hospital.

I'm so scared I'm almost having trouble breathing too.

'Keep calm,' says Scott. 'It's just the altitude – there's not much oxygen in the air so you need to breathe more to get it.'

Lily glares at him as if she wants to scream. Then she collapses onto the ground.

Scott sits down beside her. 'Take some deep breaths: nice and full. If you don't feel better we'll go down – you'll be okay as soon as we're lower again.'

Lily goes on wheezing and glaring. 'It's stupid to get this far . . . and not go to the top!'

'What's stupid is going on when your body's telling you not to. Enjoying the day is what matters, not reaching the summit.'

Which we all know is a lie; no one ever says that someone had a wonderful day almost climbing Everest or Mt McKinley, and they wouldn't say it about this mountain just because it's not as tall and doesn't have a name.

Lily stops wheezing, but she's still hunched over, breathing deep like he told her.

'You and Raven can go on and I'll wait here.'

'Okay!'

'We're not leaving your sister alone on the mountain!' Scott snaps. 'We do this as a family or not at all.'

'It doesn't matter,' Lily mutters. She's wiping her eyes with the back of her hand, and suddenly I feel it inside me: how much she wants to get to the top, and how much she hates being the one stopping us. It's probably even worse for her because she's not used to the being the one who does things wrong.

'The bears were better than getting to the top,' I say.

Then Scott pulls out the snack bags, and Lily feels better again after the dried fruit.

We're going on.

The last bit up to the head is so steep it's nearly a cliff. Scrambling up it really is proper mountain climbing. It's nearly as good as riding, except for no horses.

I pull myself up onto the bottom lip. The cliff side is hollowed out so the trail goes deep under the big beaky rock of the mountain's nose. I wave down at Lily and Scott. Scott's stopped to tighten his bootlace; I think he's taking rests for Lily.

'Not too far ahead!' he shouts. 'Don't go out of sight!'

We're nearly there; I can hardly go out of sight for more than a minute – and for once in my life, I'm going to do something before my big sister.

I wave back, and race along the ledge under the overhanging lip of rock.

4

I'm alone on top of the world.

That's why I scrambled up the mountain's face as fast as I could. I door-climbed up the steep crack beside the nose, jamming my arms and legs against the sides. Scott showed us how to do that before he and Mum even got married. I didn't know I'd get to do it on a mountain.

The eyebrow ridge was pretty flat so there was snow on it, but after that the trail curved around to the top and got really steep again. I had to stop to get my breath a few times.

Then I came around another bend – and I was on the top of the mountain.

I don't know anyone else who's climbed a mountain, except Scott. I didn't even know the word summit till last week! The highest hill in Cottonwood Bluffs is the toboggan run in the park.

And I've done it before my sister. Lily and Scott were still on the cliff below the lip when I waved to them again from the eyebrow ridge. It'll take them a while to get up here.

So for now, it's just me and the mountain.

I can see my footprints, fifteen steps in the clean white snow. It looks as if I'm the first person ever to get all the way here.

At the very tallest point there's a flat rock. I drop my pack in the snow and scramble up. Now I'm on the highest bit on the peak of the highest mountain for as far as I can see. Mountains, mountains, everywhere, and I'm on top of them all.

I'm as bubbly and jiggly as a bottle of soft drink that someone's been shaking.

I glance over at the trail. It's still safe: Lily and Scott aren't in sight. I can do my dance.

Not a choreographed jazz ballet like Amelia would do. Mine is a crazy jumping, waving my arms, spinning, Top-of-the-World Dance. Because if you can climb a mountain you can do anything.

If I had a mobile phone I'd hold it out as far as I could to take a picture for Jess and Amelia.

'This is for the best friends in the world!' I shout,

and fly into the air. Even without oxygen it's the best jump I've ever done.

I skid on the ice.

The rock tilts.

A chunk of it shatters and skitters over the side of the cliff.

Everything is in slow motion.

The rock pings and cracks as it bounces down the cliff.

I'm falling.

There's a rumble of thunder, and the earth shakes.

I don't know if I'm falling because the rock tilted or if the rock's tilting because I'm falling.

I'm skidding off the rock.

Skidding towards the edge of the cliff, arms windmilling; thumping onto my bottom.

At least now I'll stop!

I don't.

It's not slow motion at all, I'm sliding faster than the fastest toboggan, faster than an Olympic bobsledder. I'm scrabbling and grabbing at rocks and braking with my legs.

Nothing works. Nothing slows me down.

I'm going over the edge of the cliff.

White fear: a snowstorm of terror.

I'm bouncing, skidding, rolling, tumbling, crashing down the side of the mountain. Rocks and snow are skittering all around me. I'm still trying to grab and brake, but I'm going too fast and bouncing too hard.

I'm never going to stop.

I'm going to be smashed to a jelly. Dead.

The biggest thump yet. Every part of my body hits at once and doesn't bounce.

Red pain.

The world is still spinning but I think I've stopped. It's hard to tell.

And I think I'm alive. It's hard to tell that too.

I throw up, yellow yuck into the white snow.

You can't throw up if you're dead.

When Jess's cousins' horse Bitsy turned into a bucking bronco, I flew so high I had time to think, 'What if they never let me go riding again?' because two seconds earlier I'd been thinking it was the most perfect day of my life.

Then I landed. On my bottom. It hurt so much that for a minute I didn't even know where I was.

5

My face is in the snow. My head is whirling. I can't think. I don't know where I am or why. Lifting my head hurts. There's a rumbly thunder noise floating up from below me.

The last thing I remember is being afraid that Lily would laugh if she saw my Top-of-the-World Dance.

Then I see the sick in the snow. My whole body remembers the fall and nearly throws up again.

I wiggle onto my hands and knees and crawl away from the sick. The ledge is wide enough to walk on but I don't think I can get up. My teeth are chattering and I'm shaking all over. My elbows are so quivery it's hard to crawl.

I never knew elbows could be quivery.

But I never knew you could be this scared. I never

knew you could hurt this much all over.

My eyes are blurry and my face is wet: I must be crying. My glasses have fallen off. I pat the snow in every direction; my hands are so frozen and stinging it's hard to tell if I'm touching glasses or stones.

It's always stones.

'Lily!' I shout. 'Scott!'

I crawl forward; crawl backwards again because the ledge is too narrow to turn around. Doesn't seem like my legs are broken; they just hurt. I'm more worried about my glasses.

I've lost them.

Mum's going to be so mad!

Maybe she'll let me stay home from school till I get new ones.

I wiggle back against the cliff wall and push myself up. I'm afraid to move out from it; my knees are shaking too hard to trust them. My teeth are chattering so hard I keep biting my tongue.

'LILY!' I shout again. 'SCOTT!'

They don't answer. There's nothing but that low grumble of thunder.

Thunder comes from the sky, not the earth.

'SCOTT! LILY! HELP!'

Still no answer.

When I didn't want to see them, I meant just for a

minute! I'd do anything to see them again now.

I don't know where they can be, and I don't know where I am either.

This is the same sort of ledge I hiked up but nothing looks right. The cliff below me is steeper and I can't see the mountain's big hooked nose. The nose is as big as a house; I wouldn't need my glasses to see it.

It's like a movie, like walking through the wardrobe into Narnia. This can't be real.

Now you're being silly. That's real blood on your hands and legs. Real cuts and bruises. You're not dreaming, not dead; you're not in a movie.

Sometimes talking to yourself helps, if there's no one else to tell you to get a grip. I take a deep breath.

The nose couldn't have disappeared.

I've fallen off another side of the mountain! That's the only thing that makes sense.

But they should still be able to find me. The mountain's not that big at the top.

'LILY! Scott, Lily! WHERE ARE YOU?'

Now I'm just straight out screaming, and I'm getting more scared with every scream because they're still not answering – and wherever I am, they should have heard me. Scott should be running, shouting that everything's okay. Even my sister wouldn't ignore scared-just-about-to-death screams.

33

My voice is cracking. I can't shout anymore.

It's not fair! I'm the youngest!

It's all my fault: I wasn't supposed to go out of sight. Now I've lost them.

I can't see or hear or think. The fear is blacking out the sky and swallowing me up like a beam of light into a black hole. I'm nothing but a shivering, screaming speck on a lonely mountain.

So stop screaming, says a voice in my head. Not my voice, not my mum's. Maybe it's my dad's, talking to me all the way from Australia. I always knew he'd think about me if I really needed him.

I take a deep breath and burst out of the blackness. My mind is sharp and clear – and has finally remembered what Scott said to do if we got lost. '*Stay where you are and blow your emergency whistle.*'

The whistle's still around my neck, barely dented. I'm so relieved my knees fold up and drop me into the snow. I don't know why Lily and Scott couldn't hear me shouting, but they'll hear the whistle for sure. They'll use theirs to answer.

They don't.

It's an hour since I saw them. The one thing I know for sure is that even if they haven't heard the emergency whistle, they'll be trying to find me.

Unless they've fallen off a cliff too.

Don't be stupid: what are the chances of three people falling off cliffs at the same time?

They can't hear me because they're at the top! They probably got there just as I fell off it. Even if they hadn't, they'd go there to look for me.

I blow my whistle and shout once more, listening so hard my ears tingle, but there's still no answer.

Every bit of my body is bumped and bruised, and it all hurts more than my tailbone after Bitsy threw me.

'You've got to get back on,' the cousins said. 'You can't let a horse think you're afraid.'

I was afraid, and my bottom hurt more than I thought a bottom could hurt, but I rode Bitsy all the way home, and the next day when the doctor said I'd broken my tailbone, I made Jess swear she'd never tell her cousins.

I hope I haven't broken it again.

I shake a rock out of my left jeans leg and find a deep scratch up to my knee; I can't see properly, my hands are bleeding, and I don't know if all the blood is from them or other cuts I've touched. I'm cold, wet, and shaking; when I pull up my jacket hood it dumps a load of snow down my back.

But I can walk.

It's time for me to find them.

Another deep breath.

I have to get back to the peak.

The fastest way has got to be up the cliff face I've just fallen down. It's covered with bumps and cracks – way more handholds than the rock-climbing wall Scott took us to last year.

I could do it.

Maybe.

I have to. The ledge could be a dead end. I could follow it and get stuck on the wrong side of the mountain.

But that's not the real reason I need to climb the cliff. The real reason is that I'm making a deal with God: if I do something I'm this scared of, I get to find them. I have to climb it.

Except now my feet won't move. They're glued to the ledge, because my feet are smarter than me and they know that climbing the cliff is no more like climbing in a gym than being thrown off it was like sledding down a hill.

Where I absolutely agree with my feet is that I don't want to fall down that cliff twice. In fact, I don't want to fall down any cliff, ever again.

Anyway, I'm not so sure God makes deals like that. He might think the same way as Mum – and she'd kill me if I climbed a cliff on my own.

Which is quite funny since I've fallen down it once already.

For half a second I feel like smiling.

I'm never going to smile again.

I need every bit of oxygen and energy just to keep on going, and to stop myself from noticing how much I'm hurting. Hurting every step, every breath, every time I flatten myself against the side of the mountain to look all around, up and down . . .

I've seen this view before: I'm on the trail! My brains were just too rattled to recognise it at first. Or my eyes are starting to get used to not having glasses.

'Lily! Scott!'

Nothing. Not even an echo.

I can see footprints. The snow's deeper here and not so messed up. Definitely footprints – clearer and clearer the farther I go.

I step into them. My feet fit exactly, one step and

the next. They're my own prints from the way up – and they're the only ones.

A cold chill is settling around my heart, tighter and colder with every lonesome step.

But I have to go on, just in case. It's like when you lose your Girl Scout sash and you look everywhere in your room and then you have to take one more peek in the drawer where it's supposed to be, even though you know perfectly well you wouldn't have dumped everything out of every other drawer if it had been there in the first place.

So I have to see for sure, just in case I'm wrong.

I'm not wrong.

There's nothing and no one here except me.

No Lily and Scott.

No new footprints.

No Top-of-the-World Dance Rock.

No daypack sitting beside the rock waiting for me to put it back on.

And no huge rocky nose on the mountain below me. That side of the cliff is gone.

6

I can't believe this is where I did my happy dance and worried about my sister laughing.

I never thought of worrying about the mountain. After all, mountains are made of rock. They're very old, very strong, and very, very solid. Everyone knows that eleven-year-old girls can't break mountains.

Except I think I did.

Because what if the rock tipped because I fell, and if it slid because it tipped, and if it broke the mountain's nose because it slid?

The chill around my heart is turning into a solid block of ice. This is a cold, lonely, dangerous place and I'm getting out of here as fast as I can: slipping, skidding, falling, landing on my cut-to-shreds hands, sucking off the blood and snow.

The snow soothes my screamed-raw throat.

Mum says snow's full of germs no matter how clean and white it looks, but there aren't any animals up here to pee on it. I grab another handful and the bloody handprints give me an idea:

L & S
Going down trail
R xxoo

I write it in the clean white snow on the other side of where the Top-of-the-World Rock used to be. It makes me feel better, as if I know what I'm doing. I've written them a message: now they'll have to find me.

My sister will tease me about being clumsy enough to fall off a mountain; Scott will give me one of his quick, embarrassed stepfather hugs and tell me off for going out of sight when he'd said not to. I don't care: I just want to find them.

You'd think going down a mountain would be easy. It's not: it seems even steeper than climbing up. I've barely taken two steps, and I'm already skidding on loose gravel.

I swing my arms, get my balance . . . but my heart

is still thumping like it wants to jump right out of my chest.

When Jess, Amelia and I went on the Death Drop at the Cottonwood Fair, we screamed all the way down, because it felt like were going to die. Now I know we only thought it felt like we were going to die. Inside we knew nothing bad was going to happen, because my mum was waiting on the ground, and as soon as we got off we could stop being scared and go on to the next ride.

I need Mum now!

I'll try sliding on my bottom. It'll be like tobogganing with Jess and Amelia.

Pretending hard enough stops you being afraid. We're all squished on together, Jess in front because she's smallest, Amelia in back because she's tallest, me in the middle because that's the way we are. I'm not as smart as Jess or as good at sport as Amelia: I'm the middle bit that joins two long sides of a triangle, practising handstands with Amelia and writing plays with Jess.

Amelia's complaining about the bumps – she's a bit of a princess even though she's so sporty – and Jess is laughing because she's usually the one who gets scared first. 'How come you're going so slow?'

'You have to be here,' I tell her.

Just like tobogganing with Jess and Amelia – except for being alone and no toboggan.

Anyway, it's getting too bumpy for my poor bruised bottom, and my hands are burning from skidding in the snow. I'll start walking again once I've wiggled around this next big rock.

My stomach heaves at the sight of yellow sick in the snow: I'm back on the ledge that I landed on.

No wonder I didn't recognise it! It used to be the eyebrows. Now it's just a ledge of rock sticking out in the middle of nowhere.

As long as it doesn't break off too.

I scrabble along as quickly as I can, my back against the cliff. The further I go the more rocks there are to scramble over. I can't believe I ever thought scrambling over rocks was fun. That was before I knew that a mountain could throw you farther than a horse.

There's a jagged cliff where the nose used to be. The trail around it is steep; it must be where I door-climbed up. I can't figure out how to door-climb down. I'll have to go on my bottom again.

Maybe I have broken my tailbone after all.

There's a big rock at the bottom; I crawl over that,

and around to the ledge that used to be the bottom lip.

I was wrong about the mountain's whole face being gone.

It's only the lumpy part of the nose – and it didn't disappear. It just broke into three pieces and slid further down the cliff. The smallest chunk landed square on the ledge, blocking off the trail in front of me as neatly as a door; the other two huge boulders are resting on the cliff below.

Exactly where Lily and Scott were the last time I saw them.

7

'Lily, Lily . . .'

My face is pressed against the rock where the trail used to be. I'm the only one left alive and there's nothing I can do but scream.

'Lily, Lily, Lily, Lily, Lily, Lily, Lily, Lily, Lily, Lily, Lily, Lily, Lily, Lily, Lily, Lily, Lily . . .'

My throat gives up. *Gasp-hiccup-burp*. It sounds disgusting, but it doesn't matter, no one can hear.

I can't move; I'm emptied out and hollow inside, glued to my sister's grave.

'Raven! Raven, can you hear me?'

The voice is whispery and muffled. I spin around, but there's no one there.

Lily's dead and now her ghost is haunting me!

'Raven, would you stop screaming and listen!'

That sounds more like my sister. Not like a ghost.

'Where are you?'

'In here – behind the rocks.'

'You're not dead?'

'Of course I'm not dead! I wouldn't be talking to you if I was dead!'

Behind the rocks, not under the rocks! Alive, not dead; behind, not under! It runs through my head like a poem; I'm so happy that it takes me a minute to realise that behind the rocks is still not great.

When I ran through it on the way up, the trail was like a cave with the front side open. Now it's a tunnel because the two biggest chunks of the nose have only slid far enough to completely cover the front. Except tunnels have exits.

Lily's voice is coming from a crack between the door rock and the cliff. I put my face to the gap, but it's too small, I can't see her.

'Why don't you go out the other end?'

The world's stupidest question; luckily she's talking at the same time.

'It's so dark I can't see – and I can't get through to the other end. Can you see how we can get out?'

The nose rocks are huge. This one is as big as a

door; the other two aren't even rocks, they're slabs of mountain. There's no way I could move them; even Scott . . .

'Where's Scott?'

'He shoved me under the hollow when the first stone hit – it sounded like a gunshot! But the next rock got him before he was all the way in. He's breathing, but I can't wake him up.'

Her voice is trembly and that's the scariest thing of all. My big sister and stepfather are trapped; he's unconscious and she's scared. I'm the only one on the outside.

If I scrunch my eyes up tight, I can pretty well see the puzzle pieces of where these three nose rocks fitted together. I'm hoping that means there wasn't much left over to fall anywhere else.

'Lily, I'm going to go check the other side.'

I'll have to go straight across those huge pieces of nose, below where the trail used to be. The two boulders are so big and lumpy that if I slip, I'll only slide down to the next bump. Easy for someone who's already fallen off a cliff.

It would be even easier if I had a rope. I could lasso one end around that pointy bit at the top of the door rock where it juts up over the roof of their cave, and the other end around me.

But the rope's in Scott's backpack.

I probably couldn't lasso it anyway. I might as well get started and stop wishing for things I can't have.

I wish I could see better, I wish I had gloves, and I wish my hands weren't already bleeding! I wish I could have a hot chocolate with marshmallows, and I wish Mum was here and I wish Lily and Scott weren't behind the rock!

Luckily the smarter part of my brain is studying the rocks while the other part's whining. I need to slide down to the first bump . . . which doesn't seem quite so easy now I'm doing it. I hug the rock as I wiggle across: right foot slide, right hand grab; left foot slide. Slip down between the two rocks where they've split, catch my breath and study the second one. If I jump and reach high as I can . . .

'OW!'

I suck my finger till it stops bleeding: the left pointer fingernail is ripped down to the quick. *It must be called quick because it makes you jump so fast.*

What's scary is that if I hadn't been wedged between the two rocks, I'd have fallen off, because as soon as it got hurt my hand forgot all about holding on.

So when you're climbing, it's just tough luck if you hurt yourself. The only thing that matters is not falling off.

I don't know if I can remember that.

Anyway, now I've slowed down I can see there's another way up to the second rock, that doesn't need me to rip off any more fingernails. I wiggle on my stomach, across and up . . . and I'm at the other end of Lily's cave.

It wasn't just the nose that fell off the mountain.

This end of the ledge, right to the bend, is covered with a pyramid of rocks higher than my head.

But each one is a rock, not a boulder. I could move them.

If I take them down, one by one . . .

. . . it'll take days.

But what else can I do?

The pile is too wobbly to climb. I lean into it and push off the highest rock I can reach.

'OW!'

I shove the rock off my toe and over the ledge. My finger's bleeding again too. Maybe I should start lower down.

Sitting with my back against the mountain, I kick off all the loose rocks around the edges. 'Ten down, a thousand to go!'

It feels good. I'm getting somewhere.

The easy ones are gone, my legs are getting quivery from shoving, and the pile doesn't look any smaller than when I started.

There's still one big rock at the bottom that I might be able to move. I brace my back and shove with both feet . . .

I've done it! The big rock disappears over the side.

Another big one crashes towards me. I fling myself back, my knees tucked against my chest, my head thumping against the cliff wall.

The rock brushes past my toes, smashes onto the ledge, and bounces over the cliff.

The whole pile shivers behind it; rocks roll and settle. But only two go over the cliff – the rest must have rolled into Lily and Scott's cave.

8

4:05 FRIDAY AFTERNOON

Crawling back across the boulders to Lily's side of the cave makes my hands bleed more, but it's easier than telling her I can't dig them out.

I thought it was a rule: if you try absolutely as hard as you can when things are really tough, they have to work out.

That's what's fair.

It's not fair that Scott's knocked out when he's the one who's supposed to be taking care of us.

It's not fair that Lily and I are both sitting with our faces against this horrible door rock but we can't even see each other through the gap. And I don't know why I keep calling it a door when there's no way we can open it.

It's not fair that there's another stack of rocks inside the cave just as big as the one outside, and when the rocks I tried to push off the ledge smashed into the inside pile, they bounced towards Scott and Lily.

'One nearly hit Scott – he kind of twitched, but he didn't wake up.' Lily stops for a second. I can hear her breathing, as if she's trying not to cry. 'Raven, you can't try to move any more of those rocks. If the whole pile crashes in here we'll be buried alive!'

Her words hit my ears as if they're coming from a long way away, or she's speaking a foreign language; I can hear the sounds but I can't quite understand. Buried alive is supposed to mean like when I went to Sylvan Lake with Jess's family and we took turns lying on the beach, pouring sand over each other till we were buried up to our necks and it felt warm and safe.

Lily means buried alive like dead.

She means if I try to help I might kill them.

That's what's not fair.

The morning of Mum and Scott's wedding I thought I might throw up before I'd even put on my frilly blue bridesmaid dress. Lily pinched me hard.

'You're not going to spoil things for Mum again!'

'I've never spoiled things for Mum!'

'You're the reason our dad left! Mum wouldn't need to marry Scott if you'd never been born.'

Lily's still talking. My brain keeps switching off so it doesn't have to listen. I make it switch back on. I really don't want to.

'I found the torch . . . Scott's leg doesn't look good.'

'You mean it's broken?'

'I think so.'

So how's he going to get out of there and take us all home?

Every time I think things can't get worse, they do. Worse things seem to be piling up as high as the rock pyramid at the other end of the ledge.

I've been trying as hard as I can to get Lily and Scott out, but I thought Scott would sort everything out as soon as he woke up. He'd tell me how to help them move the rocks, and then he'd take us back down the mountain and drive us home to Mum.

But Scott can't even walk down the mountain himself.

And he mightn't ever wake up.

Now it really is just me and the mountain.

'I've got to get help, Lily.'

I didn't know I was going to say that. I'm a bit surprised. So's Lily.

'You've never even walked home from school by yourself!'

'I'll just go back the way we came.'

'But there weren't any houses near the lake! Just that ranch where Scott stayed when he was a kid – and his friend's grandparents are dead. That's what happens when you come out here – you end up dead!'

Actually I think the grandparents died because they were really old, not because they were climbing the mountain, but Lily's only going to get madder if I say that.

There's a long silence, and some sniffing. I think it's Lily, but it might be me too; I've cried so much I can't tell. Then there's a scratching noise, and Lily's yowling like a cat with its tail caught in a door. She's using words I've never heard her say.

'I'm trying to push my phone through, but I can't, the stupid thing won't fit!' She's crying quite loudly now. 'It doesn't even work here – at least if you had it you might have got somewhere where you could call!'

With my eye to the gap, I can see the silvery edge of my sister's phone. It's so close! She's never let me use it before – and I wouldn't feel nearly so lonely if

I could keep on writing messages. It would have to work somewhere!

I touch it with the tip of my finger, but there's no way I can pull it through. The crack is just too small.

Lily takes the phone away and puts her finger to mine. 'Finger hug,' we whisper together.

'Be careful,' she says at last. 'Don't talk to bears.'

She doesn't need to worry: I'm so full of scaredness you could put a picture of me in the dictionary. I don't need anyone to remind me to be afraid of bears, wolves, cougars, falling off more cliffs . . .

'I'm sorry,' I say.

'For what?'

'I think it's my fault: the rockslide.'

'Don't be an idiot, Raven! As if you could have moved rocks this big!'

Funny how much better everything feels with my sister sounding normal.

The cliff at this end of the ledge is too steep to go straight down. I'll have to go back across the rocks for the third time to meet the trail.

I don't think I can.

I can't go across those rocks again, and I can't find my own way down the mountain. I can't look out for bears and cougars and wolves. I can't know where to go for help if I do get to the lake.

I just can't do it.

The night before we moved, my friends gave me a going-away card. Amelia drew the picture and Jess wrote the poem:

When Raven moved to Jenkins Creek
Her friends at home did wail and weep.
For those hills are far away
From the flat lands where we stay.

But when Raven bravely mountain climbs
She'll think of friends from time to time.
So in our hearts we'll always keep
Our dearest friend on her mountain peak.

Amelia's picture is a red-haired girl on top of a beautiful green mountain: the girl looks happy, and her face isn't covered with blood, tears and snot.

Remembering her doesn't help me at all.

I'll just stay here. I'll sit outside Lily's cave and wait. When we don't turn up, Mum will call 911, and Search and Rescue will search and rescue us.

But every time I lean against the cliff, a needle of rock jabs the back of my head. I wiggle along to a smoother bit of wall but the needle's there too.

That's because it's not a pointy bit of cliff: it's a jagged arrowhead of stone, about as long as my finger, stuck firm in my braid. If my braid wasn't so thick it would be stuck in my head.

There's no way my hair would still be braided if Lily hadn't done it for me.

I don't even mind that she said it was just because it's too embarrassing to have a sister who looks like a red-haired poodle.

'The earliest we'll be home is Saturday lunchtime,' Scott told Mum. *'But don't panic if it's not till Sunday morning. The girls haven't climbed before – if there are any problems, we'll simply take another day.'*

Friday to Sunday is two days. I've got almost no water, no food, and no tent. I'm already cold and wet, shivering and teeth-chattering.

I can't sit on a rock just below the snow line for two days.

I don't know if Lily and Scott can survive behind a

rock for two days either.

Survive means stay alive.

Not surviving means dying.

'They have their backpacks,' I remind myself. 'They've got food and water, and emergency stuff.'

But Scott needs a hospital, not an energy bar.

I can't just sit outside Lily's cave and wait.

9

Below me, the mountain is endless lumpy grey on top of endless dark green. Without my glasses it's a bit smoother and not so scary, more the way I used to think mountains were.

Somewhere far below is the truck and the road that leads to help. It seems too far to imagine – but we climbed from the lake to the top in a morning; I guess I can get back in an afternoon.

I didn't tell Lily I've lost my glasses!

I nearly turn around and go back. I have to tell my sister the truth.

She doesn't have to know.

She can't do anything about it. She'll just freak out even more, and think she has to tell me not to go.

I've already worked out that I'm the only one who can get down the mountain, but it's harder to understand that I'm the only one who can decide that I can do it. It's like I have to give myself permission.

I whisper it, and then I say it out loud. 'You have to get help. You are allowed to hike down the mountain by yourself.'

I've got half a bottle of water, my watch, whistle, and a can of bear spray on my belt. My compass should be in my pocket.

No – it's gone.

I liked having the compass; I liked watching the way the needle quivers as it finds north, and I liked knowing how to use it, but I'd like it even more if I had it now.

I'd like to have my backpack too, and everything inside it. And my glasses and my Cottonwood Sluggers cap.

Don't you dare start crying again!

I dig hard through the rest of my pockets.

An apricot! The last of the dried fruit in my ziplock bag. I'd rather have an apricot than a compass anyway. I chew every last bit of goodness out of it, stow the bag back in my pocket, and have two sips of water.

I'm ready to go.

Scrabble-slide down the nose-boulder cliff, and drop to the ground. Every sore point from my ankles to my neck jolts.

I'm in the middle of a field of rocks. Broken chunks of mountain are scattered across the open slope like tombstones in a ghost-town cemetery. Walking through them gives me the shivers.

Because these rocks weren't here this morning.

How am I going to tell people where Lily and Scott are if things keep changing? What if there's another rockfall, or an earthquake?

What if I just can't remember how to get back here?

There's not even any more snow to write in. Nothing but rocks. Rocks, rocks, rocks.

If I were a cartoon figure, a light bulb would be popping out of my head.

Inukshuks! We made them in Geography last year when we were studying the Arctic. They're like a person-signpost made of rock.

I forgot that we made them out of little stones: these are proper rocks. They're heavier than they look. My scraped hands are stinging, and the torn-off fingernail is bleeding again. It's so little, but it hurts more than the big cuts; it's the only one that makes me cry.

Still sniffling, I manage to stack two rocks on top of each other – but I can't even lift the big flat one I need for the pointing arm. All I can do is find some stones and make a little Inukshuk on top of those two rocks: four stones for his legs, a long one for his signpost arm, and a square one balancing on top for the head.

You never know, someone might be hiking up here right this minute. Maybe a whole group of families has set up camp at the lake, like when Jess's family goes camping with her aunts and uncles and cousins. They'll have cars, and phones, and lots of people to help go back up the mountain and rescue Scott and Lily.

I've got to mark the way, so they'll find the cave, even if I never get down.

Jess has two grandfathers and grandmothers, eight uncles, six aunts, fifteen cousins, two sisters, one brother, a mum and a dad.

Amelia has one real grandfather and grandmother, one ex-stepgrandfather and grandmother, and one stepgrandfather; four stepbrothers and one stepsister, more step aunts, uncles and cousins than she can count – and one mum, one real dad, one ex-stepdad, and one now stepdad.

Until Mum married Scott I had two grandmothers, one aunt and uncle who live in Florida, one sister and one mum. And one real dad, but I'm only counting people I've met.

I'm the only person I know who's never even seen their real dad.

If there aren't any campers, I'll drive the truck till the phone works.

The plan must have been growing, all by itself at the back of my mind ever since Lily said there were no houses on the road to the lake. Now I've pictured it, it seems real. I can see me in the truck's driver's seat, bumping down that dirt road.

Why not? On those long two days driving from Cottonwood Bluffs to Jenkins Creek, Lily and I took turns going with Mum or Scott. Riding in a truck is different from sitting in the back seat of a car; you notice more about what the driver's doing.

The truck has gears. You have to put in the clutch to change the gears. There's a picture of the gears on the gear stick.

The clutch is the left pedal and the brake is the middle one.

The spare key's hidden just above the left back tyre – Scott said there was more chance of losing the keys on the hike than of someone stealing the truck. Of course he didn't know he was going to be lost instead of the keys.

He left his mobile phone too, in the spare esky under the bag of garbage.

All I have to do is get back to the lake, find the truck and drive till I get to where the phone works so I can call Mum.

The furthest it can be is that service station with the bear paw prints. I hope it's before that.

But the truck's still nearly a whole mountain away.

I'm at the other end of the cemetery field before I realise this is where Lily started choking. Of course the tombstone rocks weren't here this morning, because I hadn't broken the mountain yet.

Did Lily know, somehow? Was her running out of breath a sign that we should have turned around and run down the mountain as fast as we could?

The strange thing is Lily never has anything much wrong with her at all. Until she turned into a witch, she'd always been a kind of golden girl – and I'm not saying that just because she's my big sister and the opposite of me. When I was little I thought she was the fastest runner and best ball player in the world. Even now I know that's not true, sometimes I still feel secretly proud when I watch her race down a soccer field or slug a softball. Secretly proud and even more secretly jealous.

The problem with being nearly three years younger is that I never catch up; by the time I can do something too, Lily's doing something else even better. The only thing I'm as good at is riding, and that's just because I care more: Lily likes horses, but I love them.

So if anyone had tried to guess which of us would suddenly forget how to breathe, they'd have picked the scrawny, freckle-faced, can't-even-go-out-in-the-sun-without-getting-frizzled little sister, not the one who's a natural at everything she tries.

I still wish I hadn't said Okay when she said we should go on without her. I didn't mean to be the only one who got to the top after all.

10

The ridge we followed up this morning is at the end of the cemetery field. It's like the spine of the mountain's back, from here down to where we saw the bears. After that, I just have to find the trails and keep on walking downhill till I get to the lake.

I build another Inukshuk to point across the cemetery field. He's little, but I put him on a table rock sitting a little way apart: the rescuers can't miss him.

Except it's already getting harder to believe that anyone's going to camp at the lake.

I've got to get to the truck before dark.

I change my watch to mountain time: twelve past five instead of twelve past six. That gives me a bit longer till nighttime, but I don't know if it's enough.

So walk faster! says that voice in my head.

If walking faster is good, running is better. For about twenty steps all I can think about is staying on the path and not tripping on loose rocks.

After that all I can think about is how much I hurt. Every thump of my feet onto the rocky ground is a stab of pain: even my finger hurts more.

Maybe running isn't such a good idea. As long as I keep on walking, that's all that matters.

Toes numb, heels blistering, doesn't matter: keep on walking. Left, right; trudge trudge; keep on walking.

There's the raven!

It's the first living thing I've seen since I fell off the cliff.

I know it's the same one, even though its feathers were almost purple in the sunlight yesterday, and they're just plain black now that the day's getting dark. It's flying the way it was when we first saw it, flapping its wings so slowly and lazily you know it could go faster if it wanted, but this is all it can be bothered to do right now.

'Hello, Mr Raven!' I shout. That's one thing about being alone on a mountain: you can shout out anything you like.

Coyote Girl will be Jess's best play ever when she works out the ending. Coyote Girl crawled away from a picnic when she was a baby and got adopted by a coyote family.

I'm Coyote Girl. Amelia's Mama Coyote; Jess is the director and the real mother, but later on she's the hunter. She wants the hunter to accidentally shoot himself so Coyote Girl lives happily ever after, wild and free with her coyote family.

Amelia wants Mama Coyote to chase the hunter away in a ferocious but beautiful jazz ballet dance.

I want Coyote Girl to track the hunter, but he turns out to be her father and they all go home and live in one big happy coyote and people family.

The raven's gone, and I'm alone again. Alone on a mountain is different from other kinds of alone. Alone in your room is good sometimes, not when you've been sent there but just when you feel like it, because your bedroom is safe, and it's your own place.

Alone out here means that no one on earth can hear me scream. I could wave, jump up and down, spell out HELP! with emergency flares . . . and nobody would see me.

Which should be good in one way, because right now I really need to pee. The funny thing is that even though I know there's no one anywhere around, I still wish there were some trees I could hide behind.

Because I know I'm alone from people, but I'm not so sure about bears. Or wolves or cougars. Wild animals are different from people; just because I can't see them doesn't mean they can't see me.

I really don't want to get eaten by a bear while I'm halfway through peeing with my jeans around my ankles.

It's the opposite scariness from last night, because then there were lots of trees that the animals might be hiding behind, and here there are none for me to hide behind. Last night, before Lily and I went off together, Scott shone his torch into the woods and shouted, 'Hey, bears! Lily and Raven want some privacy here!'

That was something I never knew I wanted a dad for: to scare off grizzly bears so I could pee.

Anyway, I can't hold on till I get past the tree line. I should have gone in the cemetery field. It had enough big rocks for a hundred kids to find their own places to pee.

Though I like the way the mountain is starting to look almost normal, without so many newly broken rocks thrown around.

Why do you want it to look normal? Amelia asks in my head. *It doesn't make it any easier for Lily and Scott.*

Because somehow it doesn't seem quite as bad if

I haven't wrecked the whole mountain. Because half of me knows that Lily's right, there's no way my Top-of-the-World Dance could have knocked a huge cliff off the side of a mountain – *Of course you couldn't!* Jess agrees – and half of me knows I did. Knows that Scott being hurt, Lily being scared, and both of them being trapped is all my fault.

So just keep on going; that's all you can do, Jess soothes.

But pee first, or you'll wet your pants, Amelia teases.

I do what Amelia says.

That feels better. Not just because I've stopped feeling like I'm going to burst, but because I've never peed outside before without Lily or Mum watching out for me. I automatically feel braver now I have.

Maybe that's why the other voice, the Dad one, suddenly pipes up: *If you can move chunks of rock the size of a car . . . you can do anything. Even get out of here alive and rescue Lily and Scott.*

It's still too high for any bushes or normal plants to grow, but the mountain's starting to get that softer look, as if the rocks are more settled into the ground. Sometimes little tiny plants are tucked in beside them.

And up ahead there's a sticking-out rock that just about says *Raven is on the right trail*. It's the hail-shelter rock.

'You could camp here if it was bigger,' I said when we were squatting under it this morning. Which is another of those things I wish I'd never said.

'*You* could. I'd rather sleep outside again.' Which is something I wish I hadn't heard Lily say.

'Or you never know – if everything goes smoothly, we could even drive home and sleep in our own beds tonight,' said Scott.

Maybe it would have been better if nobody had said anything.

There's still a small white drift of hail against the north edge of the shelter rock. The bottom stones are dirty, but the ones on top are ice-cube clean. My mouth is so happy it could make an ad:

When you're lost and all alone
What you need is a good hailstone!

The lichens are still there too.

A terrarium seems like a pretty dumb idea now. If

Lily and Scott aren't home safe, a pickle jar of moss is never going to make Mum smile.

Suddenly I can't help it – *I hate them, I hate them, I hate them!* – because six hours ago I was happy and excited to be so far up a mountain that lichens were the only plants, and now they make me feel like a fat black F on a spelling test. I kick those pretty golden cups right off the rock and stomp them into dust.

I'm sending Mum an ESP message: *Don't wait till Sunday! Call 911, get a search party, drive up and find us!*

But Mum's not a mountain climbing, rescuing sort of person. She's more like a mum in a kids' book: she likes cooking, flowers and music – and even though she used to whack in nails and fix things around the house before she married Scott, she just did it because she had to, not because she liked it. She's too pretty and nice to be a hero.

About a year ago, the hot water heater in the basement burst. It wrecked the carpet, and the laundry cupboards got so soggy they fell apart. The landlord sent a carpenter to build new ones.

He came back about twenty times to make sure they were exactly right. Then, one night, Mum was making chili and cornbread. She always makes too much, so she asked him to stay for tea.

He stayed.

11

Here's a list of all the things I don't want to see: bears, wolves, cougars, bobcats, coyotes, rattlesnakes – and sunset.

I didn't know that sunset was on the list until the sky started turning red. Last night I loved the way the mountains turned different shades of purple, with the sky all pinky-gold behind them – but scenery is only beautiful when you're safe. Tonight sunset just means it'll be dark soon.

I've got to get to the truck first.

It's not like I've been dawdling. I've built three more little Inukshuks, but I've been going as fast as I can in between. And the faster I go the more I hurt. My body is nothing but a bunch of sore bits joined together.

Think about the parts that don't hurt.

73

That's a shorter list than the things I don't want to see:

My eyelashes.

My right eye. (The left one got dust in it.)

My left ear.

The inside of my left elbow.

There must be somewhere else!

My hair.

And my front teeth. (The back ones feel like I chomped on a rock. I probably did!)

I don't know if this is the tree where we ate lunch, but it's definitely a tree. I'm glad to see it again now, and not just because it means I'm about half way. Even skinny, deformed trees are friendlier than rocks.

Trees make shadows too, and shadows aren't so friendly. Shadows are tricky and twisty, and now I really wish I had my glasses because some of the shadows look like bears, and what if there are bears that look like shadows and I can't tell the difference?

The farther down I go the more trees there are and the longer their shadows are. The more shadows there are, the harder it is to follow the trail. It's not much of a trail anyway.

On the way up it didn't matter so much; we were going to get somewhere where we could see the summit. But the bottom of a mountain is a lot bigger than the top. There are a lot more places you can end up on your way down.

Besides, Scott was in charge. Lily and I were just looking out for animals and interesting things, we didn't have to worry about where we were going.

If I could find a lookout place before I get into the forest, maybe I could see the lake. *I'd really like to see the lake!*

Try that big stack of boulders.

My knees whine that they aren't in the mood for scrambling up any more rocks today. And that there's no point since I can't see anyway.

'Tough luck!' I tell them. 'I've got to try!'

My knees were right. It's too dark. I can see the shapes of nearby trees but everything else is a black soup. The sunset has gone.

I'm going to get lost, I'm never going to find the truck . . .

Stop panicking! says the Dad voice. *Just figure it out.*

The last of the sunset is on my left. The sun sets in the west.

The peak is due south from the lake, so the lake is due north from the peak.

Line myself up now and go absolutely straight. No zigzagging.

Another list: useful things I had on the way up that I wish I had now:

My compass.

The maps.

My torch.

Scott's GPS.

Scott.

When we left yesterday morning Mum had the boxes lined up in the living room, ready to unpack. We knew she was just itching for us to back out of the driveway so she could rip the first one open and drink her coffee in a muddle of bubble wrap and crumpled newspaper.

Of course she won't be unpacking now. She'll be at the Coffee Corner, giving other people whatever they want to eat and drink.

The truck has food. There are cans of baked beans and wieners for our dinner tonight, and apples and chocolate chip cookies for dessert. I can't remember if there are any marshmallows left. Lily toasts hers so they're perfectly gold all around but I like them best when they catch on fire, and when you blow them out they're black and blistered on the outside but sweet and gooey on the inside. If I had a packet now I'd eat them all raw, pink, yellow or white, I wouldn't care.

I don't know what I'll have first. I don't know if I'm hungrier or thirstier.

Scott and Lily have all the dried fruit, energy bars and two extra bottles of water.

It's fair that I'm the one who's hungry because everything's my fault. I'll just eat something very fast before I drive for help.

You can't even drive, Amelia says in her I-know-better voice. *How are you going to do it in the dark?*

The truck's got lights, says Jess. *Raven will figure it out.*

I'll call Mum, and she'll tell me to crawl into my sleeping bag and sleep till the rescuers pick me up. She'll say everything's going to be all right. And when she's called 911 she'll start cooking a midnight feast for when we all get home.

'All get home; home, home, home!' The words have been running around in my head for so long I can't remember what they mean. The only thing I believe in is how much my feet hurt, and my finger, my bottom, and a new scratch across my cheek from walking through branches in the dark.

And I'm tired. Beyond tired. There's not even a word for how tired I am.

The moon's coming up, and it's round and shining bright enough to see, but it makes the shadows spookier; the world is in black and white. Everything looks blurry too, even blurrier than usual without my glasses. It might be because I'm crying again. I can't tell anymore. My feet can't be bothered to lift themselves over roots and rocks and every time I trip it's harder not to fall.

Every time I fall it's harder to get up.

This time I can't. Can't get up again. I'll just stay where I am.

It's not safe here, says the Dad voice. *This is too cold; too hard; too out in the open. You've got to keep going till you find somewhere better.*

You can do it, says Jess. *You're a hero. Remember, you're Coyote Girl!*

It's hard to believe in Coyote Girl right now.

I thought you were going to save your sister, says Amelia.

Lily. I remember now: I have to get up, and I have to get to the truck.

Or that log.

The trunk is taller than my head. The skeleton of its bare roots twists into the air like a haunted forest.

Suddenly it seems like nothing in the world is safe. Mountains move when you dance on them, and trees that are quietly minding their own tree business get ripped out of the ground. Just like that, from one minute to the next, the tree's life was over, just like the bear Scott shot.

I'm shaking so badly my knees are wobbling. I'll never be safe or warm again. But in the curve between the bottom of the trunk and the roots there's a little den, with a floor of pine needles and moss. A Raven's nest.

I'm not sure if I'm lying down or falling.

Some digging-in stones wake me up before I knew I'd gone to sleep. I chuck them out, grab some moss off the top of the log for a pillow, pull my hood tighter around my face, and drink the last swallow of water from my bottle. The bear spray is digging into my other hip: I take it off my belt and curl myself around it. It's the last thing I own and I don't want to lose it.

Good night, Mum, I wish.

Sleep tight, Lily.

Get well, Scott.

Last night, when I was going to sleep by the fire and I couldn't say goodnight to Mum, I reached out to touch the end of my sister's ponytail, gently enough that Lily didn't notice but I knew she was there.

Amelia has all those stepfathers and uncles and everything but she doesn't have a sister.

Lily's crashing around on her side of the bedroom. I try to tell her to be quiet but can't wake up enough to talk. When she finally settles down she snores like a pig, and I dream about how cross she's going to be when I tell her that in the morning.

Then I tell her my nightmare about falling off a cliff and starting an avalanche that trapped her and Scott inside a mountain. I'm so happy it was just a dream that I go back sound asleep.

But I don't know why she's getting up before it's even light, and I don't know why she has to take my blankets. She's even spread gravel on my mattress which is the meanest trick she's ever played. It's lumpy and horrible and if I could wake up I'd go and get into her bed instead.

I can't wake up. I go on shivering and curl up tight like a puppy.

12

I'm lying on the ground. I'm cold right through; my neck is stiff, my bottom hurts and my legs ache – but even in my sleep I know waking up is going to be worse.

I open my eyes.

It's morning. The sun is high in the sky. I'm snuggled into the roots of a dead tree; I'm very hungry, I need to pee, and Lily is locked in a cave at the top of the mountain.

But I'm not alone.

On the other side of the log are the white mother bear and her two cubs.

I freeze.

I don't mean freeze like when you're playing statues. My body has turned to ice.

Scott's lectures race through my mind like a video

screen: *Don't run away, a mother bear with cubs is the most dangerous, don't turn your back, don't look it in the eye, a black bear that's not afraid of people is the most dangerous, don't scream, lie down with your hands over the back of your neck, no, that's grizzlies, this one's a black bear except it's white, if a black bear is aggressive you should shout and use your spray instead of lying down . . .*

My bear spray is behind my back.

Mama Bear lifts her head, grunts to her cubs, looks straight at me, grunts again and takes another mouthful of grass.

The cubs are playing tag, white Gretel chasing black Hansel . . . They're on the log. They race along it to the roots I'm hiding under, and stare down at me.

I've got the spray in my hand.

Hansel is on the root above my head. Gretel's following, bumping her brother's bottom to hurry him along. Hansel slips, swings upside down, and: 'Oof!'

I've got a bear on my chest!

He's bigger than I thought. I can't move; I can hardly breathe.

Double 'Oof!' That was me and the black cub together. The white cub was staring so hard that she fell off too, and thumped on top of her brother.

The two faces stare into mine – they're as surprised as I am.

They're playing! Just like Coyote Girl but with bears.

There's no way I could spray them.

No way I can lift my arm anyway. I let go of the can.

Hansel's patting my hair.

'Ouch!'

I was wrong. Turns out I could move: I just needed to have my hair yanked hard enough.

I can't believe I just shoved two bears off me!

Baby bears. Don't get smart thinking you could do that to their mum.

She's standing up, calling them with a clucking sort of grunt.

I grab the spray can again.

The cubs scamper off around the end of the log. There's a nest on the other side a lot like mine, with scuffed up pine needles and grass.

Lily crashing around, Lily snoring . . . it wasn't a dream – it was bears! I slept beside the three bears all night! If I had blonde hair I could be Goldilocks.

I peek through the lace of the tree roots: Mama bear is still watching me. Hiding doesn't seem to trick her at all.

She makes the clucking sound again.

Is she calling me?

I stay where I am, but take my finger off the safety catch. 'Thank you for not eating me.'

She looks at me again and ambles into the forest. The cubs follow; one blink and they're gone. If it weren't for the trail of waving branches and a steaming pile of poo, I'd think I had made the whole thing up.

I'm safe; they're gone. I put the bear spray back on my belt.

I should feel happy.

I shouldn't feel even more lonely and jealous. But the cubs have their sister or brother to play with and their mother to look after them; this is their home and they're safe.

Maybe they'll come back, and Mama Bear will look after me till I find the truck. I'll ride down to the lake on her back like Lyra on the Armoured Bear and when everyone's rescued I'll come back and be friends with the cubs.

You're crazy, you know that?

Of course I know it. This is not a new Coyote Girl play. I know that just because Mama Bear didn't mind me sleeping near her cubs doesn't mean she's going to look after me, and I know that if I'd done just one little thing to upset her this morning she could have killed me with a single swipe of her paw.

It's just that imagining playing with the cubs is the nicest thing I've thought since I fell off the mountain.

I thought-message Jess: *I need a happy ending for Coyote Girl! Right away!*

We were arguing about how to finish the play when Amelia suddenly said, 'You know your mum's going to marry Scott?'

'Mum told us she was never getting married again!'

'My mum said that last time too.'

'Mum and Scott are NOT GETTING MARRIED!'

I marched straight into the kitchen to ask Mum.

She hugged me and said, 'I'm sorry it came up like that. I was going to tell you tonight.'

All I could do was wish that my real dad would come back before it was too late and that Scott would go to Australia instead.

Now I'm just hoping he's still alive.

And wondering if Lily even knows it's morning inside that dark cave.

At least I don't have anything to do to get ready before I leave. No bedroll to pack away; no hot flapjacks to eat; no clean clothes to change into; no Insect-Off, hat or sunscreen to put on. No water to drink or clean my teeth or wash with.

I wish I'd told Lily about the deer poo I saw before she washed in the lake.

Lily's so pretty.

Picking up rocks makes my finger throb again but I need an Inukshuk on the Raven's nest log. It would be too terrible if I couldn't show the rescuers where to go.

I just wish I knew where to go now. I wish I hadn't lost the rocky ridge that we followed up from just above where we saw the bears.

But if I walk downhill I'll have to hit one of the trails we took up to the ridge.

Or not.

They were such skinny, wandery trails that we had to go single file. Scott checked them with the GPS and I double-checked with the compass to make sure we were mostly going south.

What was that thing we did at Girl Scouts to tell direction? I just wanted the badge; I never thought it was something I might really need to do when I was lost in the woods.

I'm not lost! I just don't know exactly where the lake is.

I stick a straight bit of alder branch in the ground.

Now I need to mark the top of the stick's shadow, wait ten minutes, and mark the shadow again. Then I'll know exactly which way is north.

The stick falls over.

I can't wait around for another ten minutes.

The sun rises in the east; I'm going north. All I need to do is keep the sun on my right, and head downhill. Easy.

I've only been walking for fifteen minutes, and I've found the ridge, the wonderful rocky ridge that's just like it was yesterday when the world was in one piece.

I do a happy dance, except not with my feet. Or my arms or anything else. Anyway, I'm happy.

And here's the berry field. Buffalo berries, Scott called them, which is funny when it's bears that eat them.

'Today's the day the teddy bears have their picnic!'

Then it happens all over again: Mama Bear is at the bottom of the field. Without my glasses I can't see her face, but her head is swinging in a berry-munching way. The cubs are a blur of black and white, so I guess that they're wrestling though I can't tell who's winning.

But I can see them all stop and stare at me.

Mama Bear tears off another branch. The black and white blur separates into two cubs.

Will they mind if I eat their berries, as long as I stay right up here?

I sneak a handful.

And spit them out again. They're disgusting. They taste like the word sour sounds.

But they're the only breakfast I'm likely to get.

Sure hope Scott was right they're not poisonous!

Pick another handful, and this time I manage to swallow. I don't chew more than I have to.

The bears are disappearing into the woods. 'Goodbye, bears!' I call after them. 'Thanks for sharing!'

Maybe they don't mind sharing because the berries taste so bad. Maybe they only eat them when people are watching, then sit around laughing when we try.

Four handfuls are enough – *for a berry good breakfast*, Scott would say: '*A berry good breakfast to get you back on the road.*'

And here's the road. The ridge is flattening out and turning into a trail. It's quite wide; the grass is flat; it's got to be the one that'll lead me to the lake; to water, the truck, the phone, and help. The words sing in my head as I hike through the forest; I'm sore and achy, hungry and thirsty, but I'm getting steadily closer: *water, truck, phone and help; water, truck, phone and . . .*

Help!

I'm back in the berry field.

13

It's got to be another berry field.

It's the same one: I've walked for nearly an hour in a big circle. Red stars explode in my brain. All that time and all that hurting and I'm not any closer to the lake!

'It's not fair! How could I be so stupid?'

I go on screaming until my throat feels like it's bleeding, then I cry, and finally I tell myself not to be such a baby. There's not much point being a baby if there's no one to look after you.

The right trail has to be here somewhere.

We were on it when we came out of the woods into the berry field. The bears were below us, but it's a big field and bigger forest, and I can't figure out exactly where the trail goes in.

I draw a map in the dirt with a stick.

The top of the mountain is south from the lake, but we zigged east for the waterfall, then back west till we got back here to the berry field.

So if I skip the waterfall and head straight downhill, I should end up where we started from.

The problem is I'll have to find my own trail to get there.

If I had my glasses, I could stand in the middle of the field and just look around for the trails. Now I have to walk right around the edge.

There's another trail at the north end of the field.

I hope it's not the way the bears went.

Though they might want to go to the lake too – they'd have to be thirsty after all those berries. I thought the berries would stop me from being thirsty, but they've made it worse. I don't know how the bears can eat so many without a drink. When I get to the truck I'm drinking a whole bottle of water before I do anything else. Then a juice. I'm so thirsty I can feel my throat dry all the way down – and the morning's getting hotter.

I wonder if it's warming up inside Lily and Scott's cave. I wonder if the icy feeling in my heart means that they're not okay, like my heart knows something I don't?

I wonder how long it takes to die of thirst?

All the way along the trail, bushes are bent and branches are broken.

As if Mama Bear has trampled them and Hansel and Gretel have been nibbling.

But even if the bears have been along here, they're an hour ahead of me. I'm tracking them; I know what I'm doing.

If you're not hunting you don't want to be the hunted.

I try to whistle, which doesn't quite work, and then hum, which doesn't work much either. My throat's too dry to even think of singing.

Doesn't matter anyway: my tummy's rumbling louder than I can sing. If Mama Bear and the cubs are around they'll think the biggest Papa Bear ever is growling at them.

I like this trail: it's definitely going somewhere. In some places it's worn right down to bare dirt.

There are prints in the bare dirt. Bear paw prints.

Sometimes Mum used to bring a Bear Claw home from the

Cottonwood Cafe. When I was little I was afraid to eat them in case they were real bears' claws, but now they're my favourite pastry. When we shared them, Mum ate the big toe and Lily and I got two toes each.

Bear poo, too.

Fresh poo is a little more real, and even scarier than the prints. I'm not very far behind the bears – but I don't know where else to go.

My stomach cramps so hard and so suddenly it feels like something's twisting my guts, folding me in half. All I can do is stagger along, crouched over and hugging my belly.

Another pile of poo. The bears must have eaten too many berries.

So have I.

I really wish that this tree was a bathroom.

I really, *really*, hope the bears don't turn around right now.

I feel better again.

Not for long.

This is disgusting! And it's not fair! I didn't eat that many!

Maybe this time I'll stay feeling better.

There's a strange buzzing, humming noise. It sounds like . . .

'OW!'

A bee stings me right on the tip of my nose. There are more coming . . . it's a cloud of bees: hundreds and thousands of angry bees.

I run for my life.

It's hard to run, I'm crouched over, trying to protect my face, waving the bees away; I can hardly breathe – what if I breathe in a bee?

One stings the back of my hand and makes me yelp again. A third hits beside it. They're buzzing and swarming, darting and diving, coming from everywhere to attack me.

I zigzag through the swarm; it doesn't matter where I go, as long as I'm running.

A tree root grabs my toe. I crash to the ground.

The bees buzz louder and dart in again. I'll never get away now. I pull my hood over my head and huddle my knees under my chest, wrap my arms around my face, tuck my hands into my armpits. The bees bump angrily against my jeans and covered-up head.

'Ow!' One found a gap between my jacket and my jeans. You wouldn't think every single sting could hurt so much.

Amelia's afraid of bees. She says she's allergic and that she'll die if a bee stings her. I don't know if that's true. Sometimes Amelia exaggerates.

What if I'm allergic and don't know it?

Jess said anyone could die if they got lots of bee stings even if they weren't allergic. Jess doesn't exaggerate except when she's telling a story.

'Ow!' That was the back of my wrist. I suck it and spit the stinger out. And the two other stingers beside it. My hand still hurts, and it's red and puffy. I jam it back into my armpit to keep it safe.

The noise is starting to calm down; I desperately want to peek out, but I even more desperately don't want more stings on my face.

Hardly any buzzing.

I'm not dead yet . . . maybe I'm not allergic. I never was before. Maybe six isn't lots.

But I need to pull the stingers out.

My nose feels like a fat red button. I can hardly even find the stinger.

You look like Rudolph, Amelia teases, but it doesn't help. Nothing's funny.

Squeezing it is like Lily squeezing a pimple. She hates if I watch her. At least she doesn't cry; a pimple mustn't hurt this much.

There's one on my ankle too.

I'm sick of crying, I'm sick of being afraid, I'm sick of hurting, I'm sick of huddling here. I'm sick of finding more things that I didn't even know I had to be afraid of.

But I still don't want to die.

I peek out through my fingers.

Bushes are smashed; bark and branches are thrown everywhere... it looks like I've been following a tornado!

One big old pine tree has huge claw marks ripped down it.

A bear-tornado.

I can't stop shaking. I don't know what made the bears so angry: I just know I need to get out of here.

I scramble up, stamping my pins-and-needly feet, and nearly step on something. It's sticky, dirty, with bits of dead bees and larvae... and dripping with honey.

Honeycomb!

Maybe the bears weren't angry, but no wonder the bees were: Mama Bear has ripped their hive right out of that tree and stolen the honey.

But she left this bit behind, and I don't care about

the dirt and grubs: I grab the empty apricot baggie from my pocket and shove the honeycomb in there, extra goodies and all, sucking my sweet honey fingers as I run.

At the Cottonwood Farmer's Market, Mum bought a little tray of honeycomb with three plastic spoons and a knife. The honeycomb was like tiny apartments in a building; it was clean and white in the yellow honey and didn't look like something you should eat. But the lady at the stall said she ate some every day because it was good for you, so we tried it. It tasted like honey except chewy; I ended up with a big glob of wax like dead chewing gum. When Mum and the honey lady weren't looking I spat it into my napkin.

14

The honey lady would throw this honeycomb straight in the garbage. It's not clean and white; it's all muddled up with bits of stuff that I don't even want to know what it is. I spit out the dirt and twigs, but eat everything else. *Nom, nom, bee larvae and wax!*

Honey trickles down my wrists and I pull my jacket off to lick my arms clean: honey, dirt, dried blood and all. Most of all I just go on licking honey till my baggie's so clean not even a search beagle would know I'd ever had anything in it.

It's magical Spirit Bear honey, and my stomach's feeling better already. No more disgusting diarrhoea stops. With this honey in my body I know I'll get back to the truck soon.

I'm weaving my way through the trees, through patches of shady cool and warm sun. Somehow I lost the trail when I was running from the bees. Maybe it was just a bears' bee hunting trail, not a regular down-from-the-mountain-to-the-lake trail.

You think a forest is quiet, but it's not really, not after you've been out in it for a while – especially a while like thirty-six hours, and twenty-two of them on your own. You learn to hear noises that you didn't notice at first, and you figure out that some of the scary noises aren't scary at all, and you go on listening for ones that truly might be. People say that if you're blind you learn to hear better to make up for it. Maybe losing my glasses isn't all bad. There are rustling leaves and crackling branches, birds chirping and cawing . . . and an engine kind of noise.

It's definitely not a waterfall.

It's coming from overhead, and getting louder: a hammering *thwunk thwunk thwunk*.

It's a miracle! Mum got my wish-message and sent a rescue helicopter!

For a second all I can do is stand and stare, hardly breathing, waiting to see the thing that will save us all. Then the tiredness drops off me like a too-loose jacket, and I'm jumping, waving my arms and shouting.

But I still can't see it: the forest is too thick and the

trees are too tall – and that means it can't see me either. I've got to get out into the open.

Running, waving, screaming, stumbling over rocks and roots, skidding on the steep slope . . . nothing matters except making them find me.

The noise is so loud it's hard to tell exactly where it's coming from; I'm looking up as I run; I've got to see it soon.

I don't see the hole right in front of me.

'HUHH-HUHH-HUHH!'

I land on my stomach, with the world's most vicious Chinese burn jolting through my right leg from my ankle to my hip. For a minute I think I'm going to throw up. Luckily there's not enough inside me to try.

Don't you dare be broken! I tell my ankle.

It must know I mean it, because it hardly whines at all once I get up.

The noise is definitely coming closer.

Racing again, hobbling on the sore ankle, veering around a huge rounded boulder; turning back to scramble up it, getting a bit higher. *Please, please, please let me see it from there. Please, please, please let them see me.*

It doesn't make any difference. I still can't see anything but trees, and the patch of sky straight above me . . .

. . . and a flash of silver through the treetops.

I skid down the boulder so fast my jeans are smoking. I can't give up now; there's more light ahead, as if the forest's coming to an end; soon the rescuers will be able to look down and see me.

The noise is very close.

I can see sky.

I'm safe; I'm safe!

My breath is gasping, my heart is pounding.

Doesn't matter, nothing matters except making them see me!

I trip, fall, and run again.

The noise is getting fainter. I burst out of the woods and scream at the sky.

'HELP! Come back! HELP!'

I yank my jacket over my head, waving it, an SOS flag any rescuers should zoom straight back for, but the *thwunk-thwunk* roar is already just a hum.

The helicopter is gone.

I'm going to explode.

I'm a cartoon character with a black cloud over my head and steam pouring out of my ears; I'm a volcano with boiling lava shooting out of my skull.

I'm angrier than I ever knew I could be.

Rescuers rescue people! That's what they do! They don't just have a quick glance and disappear once they've got people's hopes up!

'You meanies!' I scream at the empty sky. 'You bullies! Come back NOW!'

The sky doesn't answer; the helicopter doesn't come back.

Lost, scared, alone ... the words are a bunch of mean girls trying to make me cry: I didn't know how scared I was till I thought I was rescued. Now I'm not rescued, I can't forget how scared I still am. I don't know how I'm going to find help even once I get to the truck, because I can't drive and I don't know for sure that I can find the key or move the lever for the seat so I can reach the pedals. I don't know how much longer I can go on walking without food or water.

I'm screaming so loudly that I don't hear the watery murmur that's still there now the helicopter noise has gone. I'm so angry that even when I see the creek in front of me it takes me a second to understand what it is.

My body understands before I do. It throws itself

down on the bank, ready to lap like a dog, because it doesn't want to die of thirst, no matter how angry the rest of me is.

You'll get sick! Use your filter bottle! Jess fusses.

The water looks clean.

The lake looked clean too, till you saw the deer poo, says Amelia.

I don't want to drink deer poo. Or bear poo. I scoop my water bottle into that rushing, running, clear cool water.

I'm sure the filter didn't take this long yesterday!

Drip, drip, drip . . . Done.

I drink the whole bottle, gulp after gulp, so fast that it dribbles down my chin, but it doesn't matter, there's a whole river left. It cools the burning lava of my stomach; washes down the pine needle stuck in my throat; whooshes that magic honey into every part of my thirsty body.

It's easier to wait for the filter the second time, and then the next. I drink till my stomach is so full and gurgly I couldn't push in another drop.

I imagine a message to Jess and Amelia: *Not thirsty. Still scared, lost & alone.*

No, I wouldn't tell them that. I send them a new one:

On Lost Helicopter Creek. If you see a lost helicopter please send it back to me.

I wonder how the helicopter turned up so soon?

Maybe Mum really did get my thought message.

Maybe she loves Scott and Lily so much that she can feel they're in trouble.

I don't know if she knows exactly where we are. Scott calls it Greg's mountain, but I'm pretty sure that's not its real name.

But he showed her on the map. I remember that she laughed and said there was never much point showing her anything on a map, and he said she shouldn't underestimate herself and kissed her on the nose.

The first time Scott took us on a picnic at the Cottonwood River, Lily and I went exploring, and when I went back for a drink, Mum and Scott were kissing. I turned around and shouted for Lily to come see a frog; then I had to tell her it had hopped off, because I hadn't seen a frog all day.

Then I had to think hard as I could about frogs so I could unsee the kiss.

I still feel a bit funny when I see them kissing.

Lily kissed a boy once too. His name was Jordan and he was in grade 10 – I didn't see her but I heard her telling Caitlyn when Caitlyn was her best friend. Then

Caitlyn told everyone about Lily kissing Jordan and so Lily wasn't her friend any more, and then we moved, so now Lily's just like me and doesn't know anyone at her new school – except it's easier for Lily to get new friends because she's pretty and good at things, and nobody teases her about having red hair.

15

I know the rescuers aren't going to come back, but I still make another Inukshuk, big enough to see from a helicopter. I've been wrong about lots of other things so far.

I make it out of long skinny branches: not so much an Inukshuk as an arrow.

I wish I was an arrow and could fly down the mountain.

A little way along, Lost Helicopter Creek joins a smaller one; together they're a fast, roaring river. At the top of a cliff the new river plunges, straight as a curtain, into a pool at the bottom. The spray shimmers rainbows in the sun; the pool looks as bubbly and foamy as Amelia's mum's hot tub.

It's the secret cave waterfall.

I imagine another message to Jess and Amelia: *It's okay: know where I am!*

Ha ha. I am nowhere.

Because I know where I am, but it's not where I wanted to be.

And I don't feel very okay. I still feel emptied out and hollow: the only thing inside me is a black pit of exhaustion that keeps squirming into sick. I've got to climb down that cliff to find the trail we took yesterday.

The rocks are smooth and slippery from the spray.

A raven croaks what sounds like a warning, but I'm too busy to look: I'm crawling backwards, feeling with my toes, clinging with my fingers. Halfway down they're all cramping so badly I have to stop. That's when I look down.

The three bears are splashing in the spa pool below me.

Not fair, Bears! Couldn't you have got there while I was at the top? Not standing on tiptoe halfway down, stretched between two rocks like a basketballer reaching for a goal!

I don't know if I can climb back up again.

But I'm not stupid enough to even think about going

down. Mama Bear might decide to catch me instead of a fish.

The one thing for sure is that I can't stay here. My hands are cramping and my right leg's trembling. If I don't make up my mind soon I'll land on top of them. Mama Bear might not think that's quite as funny as when Hansel and Gretel landed on top of me.

I slip down the next bit of cliff. Mama Bear stops splashing to watch.

One more slide, and I land on the *Open Sesame!* rock. I take a deep breath, shake out my crampy fingers, and sidle around the ledge to the secret cave.

Yesterday, looking at a waterfall from the inside out seemed as magical as Alice in Wonderland behind the mirror.

Today it's so dark after the bright sun that I can hardly see, and it's damp and clammy. Maybe that's why I'm shaking so badly. Or because it's safe.

'Remember how scared you were after the helicopter disappeared?' my brain asks. 'And then you got over it so you could go on walking? Well, you're not going anywhere till those bears leave, so it's my turn now! Just so you know: you are petrified, terrified, scared out of your wits – and very, very afraid.'

Plus you're getting weirder, says Amelia. I agree.

'So quit it!' I tell my body.

My body's too busy shaking to listen. My knees dissolve into jelly, my legs fold like an accordion, and I collapse onto the floor in a quivery, shivery mess. My teeth are chattering as fast and loud as my heart, and I'm so cold I can feel the hairs on my arms standing up straight in their goose pimples.

So pull up your hood and zip your jacket!

That's a Mum voice, and she's right.

The shaking is slowing down, and I've stopped feeling like I'm going to throw up. I wrap my arms around my quivery legs, stare out through the waterfall and try to feel as strong as my crocodile-hunter dad.

The strange thing is that even though it's a fierce sort of waterfall, the more I stare through it the calmer I feel. Sometimes it's good not being able to see. It feels like being tucked up in bed with the covers over my head, knowing everything's safe in the house around me. Maybe it's just that the water's roaring too loudly to hear all those scary thoughts, but my mind is being washed as clean as a blackboard when the day's problems are wiped off for the night.

And I'm rocking, floating in the darkness . . .

. . . flying through the forest on the back of a great black bird. His feathers are warmly smooth against my skin; I lie with my arms at his neck and my feet at his tail and feel the strong, slow beat of his wings as he flies down the mountain. Trees flash past in a blur; the raven soars over creeks and chasms, I'm nestled in, snug as a baby on a rocking horse and know I can't fall.

He dips low into the dark forest, so that branches whisper and tickle. I'm starting to be afraid, starting to choke with fear . . . until a path opens like magic, guiding us to a clearing, safe and sunny. Mama Bear follows, with Hansel and Gretel tumbling behind her like twin acrobats in a circus. As we reach the clearing the two cubs stand up straight.

'It's okay,' says the white one, and turns into Lily.

For a minute I'm still so deep in the dream that I'm not sure if my sister is Lily or the white cub. I can't help looking around.

At the back of the cave there's a deeper nook with a shallow ledge. Neatly arranged on that rock shelf are a long, straight white feather with a black tip, the polished prong of an old antler, and a shiny black tooth, exactly like the fossilized shark's tooth in Mrs Thomas's science display.

Curiouser and curiouser, says Jess.

I imagine a shark swimming in here, chasing an underwater dinosaur, or whatever prehistoric sharks chased, millions of years ago when this mountain was at the bottom of the ocean. The cave feels old enough. Even the antler is so smooth and white it could be hundreds of years old.

But I don't think a deer would have ever come into this cave, and neither would an eagle.

Something from the sea, the land and the air . . .

They're good luck charms, Jess explains. *The tooth will keep you safe along the creek, the antler will guide you through the forest, and the feather will make you fast as an eagle!*

I feel as if I'm still dreaming as I hold each charm in my hands, letting the magic of the animals they came from flow into me. I'm swimming with the tide, galloping through the woods, and flying high above the mountain, seeing my way clear below me . . .

This time I come out of the dream feeling calm and sure: even my bee stings are soothed. My legs have remembered that they're made out of bones instead of jelly and my twisted ankle feels straighter.

I put the three things back on the shelf exactly where they were. I have a feeling it might be bad luck to take charms that someone else has arranged as carefully as if they were on an altar in a church.

But I can still ask them for help.

'Please, please, let me get home safe and get help for Lily and Scott. Please don't let it be my fault that the rockfall started. And please just make everybody safe even if it was.'

I peer cautiously out of the cave: the bears have finished their fishing and disappeared. It's time for me to go too. There's only one way I'm going to get out of this forest, and it won't be on the back of a great black bird.

The dream feeling stays with me just long enough to get to the bottom spa pool and check if the bears have left me any fish for dinner.

They haven't.

I could kill and clean a fish myself now if I caught one. I know that for absolutely sure. I could even eat it raw. Maybe I'm turning into a real raven.

One of Scott's jokes: *'What's worse than finding a worm in your apple? Finding half a worm.'*

Gross! groan Jess and Amelia.

Which just goes to show that my brain's turned into applesauce, because a worm in an apple doesn't sound gross at all right now.

16

Jess wrote a river play for us last year: she was Huck Finn; I was Tom Sawyer, and Amelia was Becky. Amelia's actually the best at canoeing and swimming, but she hates being a boy in Jess's plays, and since we were doing it in her back yard, the swimming part didn't matter much.

'What should I do now?' I ask them. 'Find the track we came up on, or follow the creek?'

A creek has to end up at the lake, Jess says.

You'll never find the trail again on your own, says Amelia.

'Thanks guys. I couldn't do this without you.'

I hate to tell you, says Jess, *but we're actually just in your head*.

The other good thing about staying out in the open means I can see Mama Bear or any of her uncles or brothers before I bump into them.

But it's hotter too. When I came out of the cave, I knotted my jacket around my waist to let the sun go right through me. Now my arms are red and my face is burning; if I stay out here any longer, it'll blister and peel.

I put on my jacket hood and wrap the sleeves around my head with a big knot in front. The ends droop over my eyes like a thick green fringe.

Oh, Raven, I hear Amelia saying, in her best snooty lady's voice, *wherever did you get such a fabulous hat?*

'I made it myself,' I answer out loud.

The raven hears me. 'Caw! Caw!' His head is cocked to one side: this is the funniest thing he's heard all day.

'Are you laughing at me?'

He doesn't answer, so I ask again: ' "Are you laughing at me?" said Raven to the raven.'

Suddenly I'm the one who can't stop laughing. The only thing I can talk to on this whole mountain is another raven, and the more I say it the funnier it seems. I laugh till my eyes cry, my nose runs, and my stomach doubles up in knots. I laugh till I'm too wobbly to stand and have to skid down the next lot of rocks on my bottom.

I laugh because I'm tired, hungry, and I've been walking since yesterday morning. I'm sore, bruised, lumpy with bee stings and mosquito bites, and the only bits of me that aren't sunburned are the ones smeared with dried blood. My heart is a solid lump of ice that never melts no matter how hot the rest of me gets.

I'm so far beyond scared it's on another planet.

And somehow I have to get down the rapids around this next bend.

The creek's got bored with winding gently down the hill, making a riverbank that a baby could follow. Now it's a whirling, splashing, rushing-over-big-brown-rocks creek with drowned trees tangled against its banks.

To make things more interesting, it's rolled those shiny brown rocks into three steps of short, splashy waterfalls with a little bit of creek between each one.

The last one's a Niagara.

The cliff beside it is taller, smoother and steeper than the one I fell down when I started the avalanche. But now I've found the river I don't want to leave it. It'll take me hours to hike around that cliff.

'Caw! Caw!'

The raven's so close I can almost feel the wind from his slow beating wings. His beak is open as if he's panting. He flies low and straight over the creek to the other side. I can see a black speck in the blue, and then nothing at all. But it's enough to tell me what I need to do.

The cliff is only on this side of the creek. On the other side it's a hill: it's steep, but it has grass and trees as well as rocks – I'll be able to slalom down it, even if I do some of it on my poor bruised tailbone.

And just ahead of me, where the river narrows at the first little waterfall, is a bridge.

You call that a bridge?

It looks like something built by giant prehistoric beavers who got sick of rebuilding their dam with trees and decided to fix it once and for all with a tumble of boulders. Now the lower sides of the rocks are so worn away the water flows mostly underneath. There are hardly any gaps between them, and the water splashing over the top is only a few inches deep.

The problem is that the water under the bridge is too deep to see the bottom, and swirls around in eight million different whirlpools before it gets to the next waterfall.

I can't stop staring and wondering what would happen if I jumped in. If I had a raft like in our Huck Finn play, I'd whoosh down and over the next waterfall, then the next . . .

. . . but even white water rafters wouldn't go down that Niagara.

Anyway, the bridge is easy! says Amelia. *It's twenty times wider than the fence!*

Amelia and I used to tightrope walk my back-yard fence, dipping our legs and pointing our toes gracefully as ballerinas. By the end of summer we could walk right around the garden without falling off. The last time we did it, Amelia turned a cartwheel. She landed on her feet, still on the fence. 'Dare you!' she said.

I'd barely brought my arms up when Mum stepped out the back door. 'Don't even think about it, Raven O'Connor!'

'I'll skip the cartwheel,' I promise Mum now.

The next rock's wide and flat, the same kind of reddish granite as the edge of the bank, as if it used to be part of the same piece. Stepping across the gap is as easy as stepping down from a stool onto the floor: the rock is dry, and I don't even need my arms for balance.

But the thing about prehistoric, rock-building beavers is that they've got a sense of humour. *See, you can do it*, they tease, making sure that the next rock's nearly touching the second one, except that it's tilted on its side, and the one after that is tilted the other way. And the spray's getting splashier, running over the top of the slippery rocks.

Just like walking the fence and running through the sprinkler at the same time.

The next rock is small and tippy, and the only way to keep my balance is to keep on going.

Don't think about falling!

Move fast, jump over foaming white water, onto the last rock. It's flat and solid and now there's just one more giant step to the other side. Take a deep breath . . .

. . . into the world's splashiest, scariest, back belly flop.

The river thumps me hard between the shoulders. It whacks the breath right out of me; I'm gasping, gurgling, and going under, blind in the frothing water. The whirlpool is dragging me wherever it wants; I can't tell which way is up and I can't go on fighting . . .

No! No, no, NO! I don't want to die!

Kicking and thrashing, I fight my way up. My fingers hit rock. There's still no air; my lungs are going to burst.

I'm upside down!

I somersault and kick off from the rock. This time I break through the surface into fresh air. I gasp it in, spit out water and sick; my lungs hurt as if they've already forgotten how to breathe.

Tread water, keep your head up!

I'm trying, I'm trying, but the creek's swirling me down towards the next waterfall . . .

. . . and over it, tumbling under the water again, spinning in the whirlpools, kicking through spray.

I'm only two metres from the shore. If I could just catch my breath . . .

Too late.

That was the last little fall before the Niagara, and fighting my way up again has taken my last bit of air. I'm whirling like a leaf; the bank is still only a couple of metres away, but it might as well be a hundred. The current's never going to let me go.

I take a deep breath: I'm going over the edge.

17

ABOUT 4:10 SATURDAY AFTERNOON

I'm under the water, spinning like a rag doll in a washing machine . . . 'OOF!'

Someone's thumped me in the stomach. Grabbed me and hauled me out.

Black spots dance in front of my eyes.

I can't see or think or hear. Can't do anything except throw up. I've swallowed litres of river, and every drop of it is shooting back up again. Stuff's spurting out of my nose too; my stomach's cramping and the rest of me feels like a giant's punching bag.

And I'm alone. It's a tree that saved me: a dead, fallen-over tree with its roots on the bank, its branches in the river, and me slumped across its trunk in between.

I must have pulled myself up when I hit it. I don't know how.

But I'm still in the river, at the top of the Niagara waterfall.

The scariest thing of all is that wiggling a couple of metres along a log is the hardest thing I've ever done. I never knew that you could be truly too tired to do something that you desperately needed to do to save your life.

But finally – wiggle, gasp, rest, cough, spit, rest, wiggle, gasp, rest – that poor soggy rag doll flops out of the washing machine onto the bank.

I've caught hibernating sickness from the bears.

I don't know how long I've been lying here, with my face against a rock and my feet still in the water. Every time I try to get up I go back to sleep again before I can move. Most of me is clammy and cold, shivery and achy, my head's as fuzzy and light as fairy floss – but the back of my tee shirt is almost dry and my neck is hot.

'*You nearly drowned!*' says Jess.

'*But you didn't!*' says Amelia.

They sit beside me so I can go back to sleep.

Time to get up!

Jess and Amelia are gone. I've got to get out of here – what time is it anyway?

My watch is smashed. The whole face is shattered away.

Not my watch too! How am I supposed to tell the time with a dead watch?

Quick: unthink the word dead.

The watch doesn't matter. It doesn't even matter what time it is, as long as I get to the lake before dark.

No time to waste: that's the only time that matters.

I'm shivering again, but my jacket's gone. That's what happens when you fall into a river with your jacket on your head.

You'll warm up when you get moving.

The three bears are on the other side of the creek; I wonder how long they've been watching me sleep.

I wonder if they could see Jess and Amelia.

Hansel and Gretel stand up, waving. More likely they're chasing butterflies or bees but I wave back, and for just a second I don't feel so cold and alone.

Mama Bear stops grazing to stare at me.

I think it's a friendly, 'Glad to see you got out of the

river alive!' stare, but it could be, 'Glad we've saved you up to eat for dessert!' Whichever it is, I'm glad it's from the other side of the creek, and I'll be even gladder when it's, 'What's that speck in the distance?' I love Mama Bear when I can't see her but she's scary when I can.

I check the bear spray on my belt: the lid's cracked but still on, and there's only a small dent in the can.

My emergency whistle is somewhere at the bottom of the river. I liked having it too, but so far I've had an awful lot of emergencies and not much good from the whistle. Next time I'll bring a Rescue Whistle.

A raven's feather, black and shiny. I've been lying on it all this time.

It's a sign: my very own good luck charm. The bears have said goodbye, and now my raven is showing me the way. Maybe it was the raven who pulled me onto the log.

I weave the black feather through the snarl of wet hair that used to be a braid, and start down the hill.

If I wasn't so tired, my head so woolly and my jeans and socks so saturated; if I wasn't hungry, lost, scared and hurting, this wouldn't be a horrible walk. But I am, so it is.

And it's steep. Bumpy-on-my-bottom, burning-on-my-hands steep; jamming-my-toes-against-the-fronts-of-my-boots, aching-fronts-of-my-legs steep when I stand up again. If the mountain had to fall down I don't see why it couldn't have got a bit flatter at the same time.

But if I follow the river, every steep step is taking me closer to the lake.

'Because I'm *not* going to get lost!' I shout.

At the bottom of the hill, the river crashes onto another heap of boulders, but this time the rocks are in the middle and the river splits to flow around them.

Now it's two creeks separated by a tongue of land.

I'm not crossing it again. I'll stick with the creek on my side.

I just wish it wasn't starting to ramble away out of sight of the main creek – but it's still flowing, it's still got to end up at the lake. I'm definitely getting closer: already the ground isn't so rocky and the forest is getting thicker, the way it was when we started out.

I spy with my little eye something beginning with T, I imagine to Jess and Amelia.

Tree, they say together.

I spy with my little eye something beginning with M.

They're stumped.

More trees! I tell them.

I'm going crazy.

The alder trees are crowding and whip-you-in-the-face springy; tangling and laughing because I'm trying to get around a steep bit of cliff, and now I can't tell which way to turn to get back to the creek. I don't know if it's in front of me or behind – or maybe I'm going around in circles: I don't know.

'Stop it! You can't lose a creek!'

The forest is shocked into silence. Then birds start chirping; a branch rustles . . . and under the quiet everyday life of the woods, I can hear the murmur of running water. The creek's reminding me that I can't hear it when I'm screaming, but that if I calm down and listen, it will call me to it.

'I'm not leaving you again,' I tell it when I've finally pushed my way through the maze.

The creek doesn't care. It's even forgotten how impatient it was to get to the lake; it's getting slower and lazier.

And wider. I'm wading in water up to my ankles: the

creek is spreading out and turning into a marsh. I must be getting closer.

The grass at the campsite was springy and green. The water at the edges of the lake was so clear and shallow you could see every pebble, but as it got deeper the colour did too; in the middle it was as turquoise as the Navajo ring Scott gave Mum. Diamonds danced where the sun hit the ripples. When I waded into it the water was cool, and the pebbles rolled under my toes.

Mud squelches under my feet, sucking at my boots. Mosquitoes scream because there's not enough room on my face for all of them at once.

I can't pretend any longer. I'm standing in a marsh. There's a small pond in the middle, but the rest of it is about the marshiest marsh I've ever seen.

It's nothing like the lake we camped on.

My legs fold. I hit the ground.

I don't understand.

I've made it all the way down this mountain, all by myself, with nothing to eat or drink and no one to look after me; I've fallen off a cliff, wrestled with bears and nearly drowned in rapids. I don't even know if I'm me anymore.

None of it makes sense if it's not the right lake.

If I squint I can see across the pond, and the marsh. I can see the tall reedy grass with its roots in the mud and its spears above the water, and the floating clouds of white scum around my feet.

Even with my filter, I won't be filling my bottle here.

After the taller grass the deep forest starts again, on and on in every direction, with the endless mountains circling around it all, and me a speck in the middle.

The sun's beginning to set, but knowing which way is west doesn't matter any more, because I don't know if the lake is east or west, north or south.

I'm lost.

Lost, lost, lost. I'm so lost and alone there needs to be a new word for it: Lostalone. Lonelost.

I'm lonelost.

No one's going to save me now. The rescue helicopter's given up and gone somewhere else to rescue someone that they can see.

I'm going to die out here and be eaten by wolves, then the bones they leave will get crunched up by coyotes. There won't be one atom left of the girl who used to be me. Jess will never be able to finish her play. Lily and Scott will starve to death inside the mountain. Mum will never know where her family has gone.

In the end we turned Coyote Girl into a game. All through July, the three of us walked around the block after dinner, as late as we were allowed, howling like coyotes. We imagined people running to lock their doors so the wild animals couldn't get in. We felt wicked, and brave.

But one Sunday Jess's family took us for a picnic at the river park. We wandered away from the flat greenness to explore the ravine: it was wild, steep and bushy. We crouch-ran through it, hiding and howling.

Somewhere down the river, a cougar screamed.

We didn't play the howling game much after that.

Tears run into the hollows around my nose and drip down my chin like the creek rushing around boulders and down the Niagara.

There's no point in going on, but I'm still folded up on the ground and the mud is seeping into my pants. It's wet and revolting; my ankles are slime grey, and so are my hands. Mosquitoes swirl in a screaming grey cloud; the only good thing about this place is that they can't bite where I'm covered with mud.

I slop up handfuls of the world's most disgusting Insect-Off; slime trickles through my fingers, oozes down my arms. It stinks bad enough it might even keep away wolves. I rub another handful onto my hair.

But there's a limit to how long you can sit in mud, no matter how much it stinks. I've got to find somewhere drier to be lost in.

Ahead of me is the corner of a fence.

A fence has to go somewhere.

'Hang on, Lily! I'm going to get you out after all!'

18

SUNSET, SATURDAY EVENING

If I ever made a calendar, I'd skip the mountains and sunsets and fill it up with pictures of this fence: this real, made-by-people, barbed-wire fence.

I put my hand flat on the top of the post, and the rough wood tells me I'm strong enough to make it to the next one. All I have to do is keep on going, post by post, without worrying about north or south or uphill or down; the fence will take me to where people will be.

My muddy boots squelch along beside it singing, 'Follow the fence, the beautiful fence; follow the fence to help!'

Sometimes I ride in the body inside those boots: *trudge, trudge, squelch, squelch,* but most of the time my fuzzy mind is so light that it bobs above me like a balloon.

'Poor thing,' my mind says, because the girl below me looks exhausted. Her muddy head's bowed, her jeans are torn, and I can tell that those dragging feet are bleeding inside their slimy boots.

I feel so sorry for her I start to cry.

Then I realise the girl's me, which makes me laugh – in a gurgly, drippy hiccupping kind of way.

The forest ends and fields begin. Way in the distance there are horses or cows; I can't see which. When I was little I thought Lily must love horses even more than I did because even if they were really far away she could tell if they were horses or cows. Then I got my glasses and I could too.

Jess is trying to tell me something important but I can't quite hear her. It's like seeing something on TV on when you're doing something else – you know it's there but you don't quite see it.

Another fence runs into mine from the right.

I keep going straight. If I crawl through it to the other one I might never get up again.

There are horses in the next field, close enough I can tell. I like horses; I remember that like something I used to know. But all I care about is getting to the next post.

It's dark. There are no stars and no moon, just black night.

Noises start: rustling leaves and creaking branches; a stick snapping. A howl in the distance; a yip, and a screech. Panting.

Cougars and wolves; coyotes and bears: they're all around me, all through the woods. They're hunting, and I'm their prey.

The hairs on my arms are standing up straight; my teeth are chattering, and my heart is thumping so hard it hurts. Every animal on the mountain must be able to hear it. I can feel them coming through the shadows, circling around me; closing in on me with sharp fangs and claws.

With my left hand I grab a stick, a branch as thick as my wrist and as tall as me. Now I've got the fence on my right side and a stick on my left.

The fence turns a corner, and so do I. Three posts along, it hits a wall.

That's what Jess was trying to tell me! If there are horses or cows, there's got to be a barn somewhere.

In the middle of the wall there's a door with a sliding wooden bolt. I slide the bolt and push the door open. It's pitch dark inside and smells like hay. I don't even bother saying hello; I can tell there's no one here.

I bolt the door behind me and scuff across the floor till my foot touches hay.

The hay smells of summer dreams; when it prickles my face I only wake enough to turn and snuggle in again like a mouse in a tissue paper nest. I don't know how many times I do that; I don't know which dreams are dreams and which ones really happened. I just know I'm safe and want to go on sleeping.

But even in my dreams I know it's morning, and when I open my eyes and see the dust dancing sunbeams through the hayloft window, I remember where I am.

I'm very tired. I'm exhausted, worn out, dog-tired, all in, wrung like a dishcloth. I'm thirsty and starving, my mosquito bites itch, my bee stings burn, my cuts hurt, my muscles are sprained and my bones ache.

But across from my hay-bale bed I can see an open door to a tack room. And inside that tack room is a big tub labelled OATS.

I stagger across the barn floor as fast as my spaghetti legs will carry me. It takes a second to knock the tight lid off the tub, but then I'm leaning over it.and digging in, cramming fistfuls of oats into my mouth.

They're not smooth like the rolled oats Mum cooks for porridge; they're the whole hard little seed kernel hammered flat, so they're nubbly and hard to chew. Trying to swallow them without chewing is worse, scratching all the way down my throat. I cough like a sick dog. The oats spray disgustingly across my front but I choke another handful down anyway.

Now I really need water. There's got to be a tap around here somewhere. Maybe outside.

I shove the bolt across to open the barn door. The bright sun is blinding, but I don't care because the tap is right there beside me, and I've already turned it on and am crouching over it, guzzling in that clear cold water. Water's running out of my mouth and down my chin but more of it is going in, washing those nubbly oats down my throat, filling up my thirsty body. I don't stand up till my belly feels fat and gurgly.

I'd almost feel sick except that my eyes have got used to the brightness now and what I can see is too exciting for sick. Because I've just realised the other half of what Jess was trying to tell me last night.

She's right: you can't have a barn without a house. It's funny that I didn't see the lights last night, because there it is, set back amongst the trees on the other side of the corral. This is what my beautiful fence was leading me to: a house, with people, and help.

I try to run. The water in my stomach sloshes and gurgles, churns and rumbles. Then it explodes. The unchewed oats spew out. I didn't think they'd even been in there long enough to turn into vomit, but it's real, stinky, yellow, cramp-in-the-guts throw-up. And it keeps on going till stars and black holes dance in front of my eyes.

My legs have turned back into soggy noodles. My head's as floaty as a birthday balloon. I'm going to fall down.

So walk against the fence, says the dad voice. The corral fence is wood, not barbed-wire. I veer towards it.

Blackness.

Blackness and peace.

Blackness, peace . . . and warm breath against my face.

I'm staring up at the bottom rail of the fence and into the deep brown eyes and white face of the horse nuzzling my neck. His rubbery lips move along me to find a pocket.

'You think I've got an apple for you?' I ask him, except I don't feel strong enough to say it out loud. 'I wish I did! I wish I had a whole bag of apples and carrots and sugar lumps, and you could share them with me.'

Apples are juicy and crunchy. I like apples. Apples are sweet and juicy, not like nubbly make-you-throw-up oats. If there'd been apples in the barn I'd be knocking on the house-door now instead of lying under this fence. But there weren't, so I go on lying there and thinking to the horse.

'What else do you like?' I ask. The horse doesn't answer – but some smarter, knows-it's-got-to-survive part of my brain does. *Get up and get to the house!*

Except it's so peaceful lying here, staring up at the sky and the white horse, that I really can't be bothered.

That's okay, soothes Jess, *you deserve a rest.*

Don't be stupid! shouts Amelia. *You can't quit now!*

That's the voice that makes me roll out from under the fence and pull myself up again. It's the voice that makes me keep on walking towards the house on my wobbly legs.

They get slower and wobblier as I get closer. Not just because I'm wondering whether these people will be the sort of strangers who want to help a lost girl rescue her sister, or strangers you shouldn't talk to. It's more because I need their help so badly I can't bear it not to be true, and the closer I get the more afraid I am that it's not true.

The house is definitely real – if I were imagining a house right now it would be Hansel and Gretel's gingerbread house with candy on the roof and icing dripping down the walls, and I would nibble, nibble like a mouse. This is a rambling, run down old farmhouse with a weather-beaten porch and a tyre swing in a big maple tree.

It's just the people who mightn't be real. I can't see anyone moving around inside.

Maybe they're asleep.

I'll have to wake them up, and that might make them so angry they won't want to help.

I lean on the door, catch my breath, and knock. Quietly.

Nobody answers.

I pound louder and louder, until I've walked right around the house hammering on every door and shouting below every shut-tight window, and no one has come out to see why. And they're not going to: there's no car in the driveway. There's no one home.

The doors are locked.

So are the windows.

I pee behind a tree, even though no one would see me if I'd peed right on the front lawn. Even my raven and the bears have given up watching me.

Then I climb into the hollow of the tyre swing, and cry and rock till I nearly throw up. My head is so fuzzy and my legs so limp that I don't know if they're going to remember how to walk.

But that's what they have to do. That's their job: to walk until I get help. It's not something I have to think about or decide, it's just the way life is. Just keep on walking. Back to the barn and down the driveway; at the end of the driveway there'll be a road, and the road will somehow lead to help. Just keep on walking.

Now even the barn looks so far away I can hardly see it, infinitely farther than it was when I came out of it this morning. That's what infinite means: however far I walk, there'll always be another kilometre before I get to help.

There's got to be another way.

I stand on tiptoe to look through the kitchen window. It's clean and tidy. There's nothing on the table or the benches. It hardly looks as if anyone lives there.

They've got a tyre swing: they've got kids. People with kids would understand if someone else's kid went into their house and used their phone to save her sister and stepfather's lives.

My heart's hammering and my mouth is even drier than when I woke. I've never done anything this bad on purpose.

I pick up a rock and whack the kitchen window as hard as I can.

The glass explodes.

19

SOMETIME SUNDAY MORNING

The hole is a jagged star, with knife points of glass. I smash those tall peaks off with another rock.

Tiny splinters of glass jump into my fingers. I'm sucking off blood, spitting out glass. My lips are bleeding too, but I don't know how else to get all that glass and blood out of my hands. I think I've swallowed a piece.

And there are still slicing-sharp ridges of glass all along the bottom of the window.

It would be really stupid to bleed to death before I got to the phone – and that's what's going to happen if I drag myself over that glass.

Half an hour ago I probably would have started crying again. But it seems like whacking that rock through the window pushed the restart button on my frozen brain.

I drag a cedar picnic chair over to the window. I turn it so its back is against the wall. Then I go back to the front door and grab the doormat. It's heavier than it looks – one of those brown bristly mats with WELCOME in black letters. I hope the welcome still works through a window instead of the door.

I heave it across the windowsill. It sticks out a lot; it's not very bendy.

Then I climb onto the chair. I lean onto the wobbly doormat but I can't pull myself up and I'm still not quite high enough to wiggle through.

Fear-butterflies flap in my stomach. I lean further onto the mat and step onto the back of the chair.

The chair wobbles and tips. There's a crash as I kick free, and now I'm lying across the windowsill doormat, scrambling forward and tumbling headfirst into the kitchen sink. The mat skids off to the floor, but my right knee smacks the edge of the draining board and I'm stuck in the sink in a jumble of hands, legs and arms. All the bare bits are bleeding. Seems like quite a lot of glass landed in the sink ahead of me.

Then my arms and legs figure out how to untangle themselves, and I swing my legs over the bench and slide onto the floor.

There should be flashing lights and prizes. There should be clapping and cheering. I've won.

The prize is a phone. That's what the ad said: 'One Free Call with Every Broken Window.'

I crunch across the broken glass on the kitchen floor. The phone's not in the kitchen.

It's not in the living room.

Now I really feel like a burglar . . . but it's not in the bedrooms either.

There's no phone in this house.

'Stupid, stupid people!' I scream at the empty kitchen. 'How could you not have a phone!'

I swing open a cupboard door, and there it is, right up on the top shelf with the cord wrapped around it. It's pathetic and useless, and even worse than no phone at all, except it means I don't have to go on looking.

There are glasses and mugs on the shelf below the phone, but the next shelf has a jar of instant coffee, a jar of tea bags, a plastic container of powdered milk and a biscuit tin. There's a full packet of chocolate-chip biscuits in the tin.

Maybe these people aren't so bad after all.

Chocolate-chip biscuits are a whole lot better to eat than raw oats. Drinking from a mug is a whole lot easier than a tap. In about two minutes I've eaten six biscuits and I don't even feel like I'm going to be sick.

Biscuits in my tummy,
Chocolate in my brain,
It's really very funny
When you think you're going insane.

That one's for Jess.

But by the time I've eaten the next biscuit I've got a plan – and that's for me.

I close the door carefully behind me when I leave the house. I guess it's a bit late to lock it with the kitchen window smashed open, but at least it'll stop any bears from wandering in.

The white horse watches me, nickering softly as I walk towards his corral.

His eyes are so big, so soft and brown, that the longer I stare into them the more I know this horse understands me. He must – he saved my life!

My plan seems better and better.

I tickle the swirl of hair on the middle of his forehead.

'You still think I've got a treat for you?'

His velvet nose nuzzles my pocket.

'What about a handful of oats?'

The barn's not nearly as far away from the house as the house was from the barn. Everything seems better when you're not throwing up.

I go back into the barn, and through to the tack room, with that happy smell of leather and horses. As well as the tub of oats, there are two saddles, two bridles and two halters; brushes, curry combs and hoof picks; linseed oil, leather cleaner and rags and a bunch of plastic buckets.

Now that my brain's working again, I notice the clipboard above the sink. There's a pen stuck through the clip and a note on the board.

RODE BOUNDARY FENCE WEDNESDAY – ALL WELL.
FED SNOWBALL AND COCOA.
SEE YOU SOON, CHERYL.

Snowball! That's got to be the white horse.
I like knowing his name.
I write a new note for the clipboard:

SCOTT AND LILY ARE TRAPPED UNDER A ROCKFALL AT THE TOP OF THE MOUNTAIN. PLEASE PHONE 911 AND ALSO CALL JENNY ON 456 6545.

I am borrowing Snowball. I will bring him back when I've found help.

Yours sincerely
Raven.

PS I'm sorry about the window. I have eaten some oats and biscuits too. I will pay you back.

20

A LITTLE LATER SUNDAY MORNING

Snowball's saddle has got to be the one with white hairs on the blanket.

It's so heavy I can barely lift it.

I need that saddle!

But it doesn't matter how much I grunt and strain, I can't swing it off the stand. I'll never be able to get it on his back.

I've always wanted to try riding bareback. Looks like I'll get my chance.

I take down the bridle hanging above it. The curb bit seems big and cold, and I don't know if Snowball will want it in his mouth.

The brown horse watches from the other side of the corral as I come out of the barn. I start rattling the oats.

Snowball comes right away, his neck stretched towards the bucket.

'That's why you're fatter than Cocoa!'

I loop the reins over his neck so he can't run away, and let him nuzzle oats from my hand. His rubbery lips tickle my palm; I'm so excited I can hardly breathe.

'You'd like to take me for a ride, wouldn't you, Snowball?'

Looking deep into those brown eyes, I blow my own breath gently into his nostrils, so he'll know and trust me. He nibbles at the hay sticking out of my hair, and snorts.

'I know I stink, but I really am a girl. Honest.'

Another handful of oats makes him believe me, so while he's chewing, I slip the bit into his mouth and the bridle over his head; do up the cheek strap, straighten the brow band . . . and he's perfect.

It's the first time I've bridled a horse.

'Thank you,' I whisper, and lead him through the corral gate. My hands are so sweaty I have to wipe them on my jeans before I can lock it behind me.

I'm stealing a horse!

It's not too late; I could lead him straight back into the corral and no one would ever know that I was nearly a horse thief.

I loop the reins around his neck again, gather them

in my left hand and line him up beside the fence.

It seems like part of me's flown free of who I thought I was. I can hardly remember the Raven who was afraid of what her sister would say, and who thought being wicked meant putting salt in Scott's coffee. This new Raven is a bruised, limping, bleeding, filthy, stinking, window-smashing, biscuit-stealing horse thief. The Raven who dances on mountain tops and treks down them on her own. The Raven who'd do anything to save her family.

Remember Bitsy? says Jess. *What if he's a bucking bronco?*

Don't be stupid, Amelia laughs. *Nobody calls a bucking bronco Snowball!*

I climb onto the fence and slide onto his back.

Snowball is round but his backbone is pointy, and luckily, his mane's long enough to hold onto. He prances around a little, just to show me he can.

'I don't care if you throw me once we find help,' I tell him. 'As long we get there!'

He tosses his head as if he'll have to think about it.

'It's okay if you don't throw me, too!'

But the head tossing and eye rolling isn't about a skinny girl on his back: it's about what's coming in the sky.

The Rescue helicopter! I've got another chance!

Snowball's sidestepping and skittering. By the time I let go of his mane to wave, the helicopter's gone. If they see me at all, they'll think I'm waving like a five-year-old at a train.

'Dumb kid,' they'll be thinking. 'Does she think Search and Rescue has time to wave at kids on ponies?'

But with a horse under me and chocolate-chip biscuits inside me, I've remembered how to hope. I'll be ready if the helicopter ever comes back – or maybe by then I'll have found the truck and the phone by myself.

I stroke Snowball's neck till we're both calm, then turn him down the driveway.

The brown pony's galloping up and down the fence, whinnying wildly.

Snowball only turns his head to whicker once. I don't know if he's saying, 'It's okay, I'll be back soon,' or '*Nyah, nyah*, I'm going out and you're stuck at home!' He can be as rude as he likes to his friend, as long as he's nice to me. Bareback riding is slippery, the drive-way is long and twisty, and I want to stay on as long as possible. Luckily right now Snowball just wants to walk. Slowly.

'Next time we'll go faster,' I promise.

There's not going to be a next time! You just better hope you get to the end of the driveway before his owners see you stealing him!

No, wait . . . that would be good.

It's hard to remember that even being arrested would be a good thing as long as I get to call Mum.

At the end of the driveway is a faded wooden sign of a galloping pinto.

It's the one Scott showed us on Thursday.

I'm on the road to the lake! This time nothing can go wrong. I won't have to drive the truck; I'll just grab that mobile phone and gallop down the road for help, like Paul Revere in the American Revolution, telling his friends that the British were coming.

Not long now! I think to Lily and Scott.

Everyone in the family came for Mum and Scott's wedding: Gram, Aunt Carol and Uncle Jason, Mum's cousin from Nova Scotia, Scott's mum and dad who I guess are sort of our grandparents now, Scott's brother and his wife and their sixteen-year-old twin daughters, his sister and her two little boys, and a bunch of cousins and their families.

Scott and his brother were standing at the front of the church.

We started down the aisle, Mum in front and Lily and me a step behind. Scott turned to watch, and I knew he was thinking that Mum was beautiful, because she was. Her dress was beautiful, and so were her flowers, but most of all, her face. She looked happy like I'd never seen her.

And then Scott cried. I never knew men could cry.

The helicopter noise starts suddenly, low down and straight ahead, as if it's landed and is taking off again. I scrunch my eyes as tight as I can, but I can't see it. The good thing is that I'm too busy hanging on to get upset.

The road ends. We follow the track past more NO HUNTING signs and into the woods.

Driving down this trail in the truck, the trees seemed to be closing in on us, warning us we didn't belong. Now the leaves and branches are blurring and soft, and the horse and I are part of the forest. I can't hear the helicopter anymore; the world is still and quiet. I click to Snowball. This time he breaks straight into a canter, an easy cowpony lope.

It's as if we've been riding together forever. I can feel the muscles moving in his shoulders and the drumming of his hooves on the ground; my legs grip the warm barrel of his body and settle into the rhythm of his canter. It could almost be a dream, except I'm breathing in the warm smell of horse and I know it's real.

Now my raven is flying in front of us, guiding us through the cool green tunnel into a dazzle of sunshine. My dream in the cave makes sense now. Everything will be all right.

I can see Scott's truck, still safely parked in front of the rock pile at the other side of the clearing.

Down from the truck, closer to the lake's edge, is a huge old log nearly as big as the one I slept in with Hansel and Gretel. A black shape is tightrope walking along the top.

Something white leaps on him and knocks him to the ground. I can see the black and white blur as they tumble in and out of sight: it has to be Hansel and Gretel. I can't believe how happy I am to see them one last time.

No, no, no!

Lying under a tree, a man in a red plaid jacket is steadying his arm against a root, squinting down the sights of a rifle at the cubs.

Snowball pushes his front legs out hard and skids to a stop. I fly straight over his head.

I land on all fours like a bear. By the time I scramble to my feet, all I can see of Snowball is a flash of white disappearing down the track.

Another flash of white is coming down the hill towards me.

That's why Snowball bolted.

It's the second time in three days that the world's changed from fairytale to nightmare.

I'm between a charging bear and a man with a gun.

21

STILL SUNDAY MORNING

'STOP! PLEASE STOP!'

I don't know if I'm screaming at Mama Bear or the man. Both.

It doesn't matter. The hunter's wearing earmuffs – he can't hear me.

I grab a stone – but what if I make him jump as he squeezes the trigger? What if he misses the cubs and hits me? And if he turns around he'll definitely shoot their mother. She's getting so close he can't possibly miss.

But the great white bear galloping through the woods isn't the gentle Mama Bear that let me sleep next to her cubs and left honey for me to find. This is a ferocious animal protecting her young, and the man on the ground might have a gun, but what he doesn't know is that right now he's the one being hunted.

She's moving fast.

The scream bursts out of me, flapping birds up from trees, freezing the cubs behind their log, and even shuddering the hunter and his rifle.

The only thing it doesn't stop is Mama Bear. She shakes her head – and keeps on coming.

The can of bear spray is out of the holster and in my hand. I don't even know how it got there.

'NO! Go back! You can't kill people!'

I'm pointing the can at Mama Bear. She's ten metres away, and I can hear the terrible clicking of her chattering teeth.

There's no way out.

I've released the safety catch. My finger is on the nozzle.

'You're blocking my shot!' the hunter screams.

I'm frozen in place; I couldn't drop to the ground even if Scott had said it was what I was supposed to do.

'She'll kill you!'

'STOP!' I shout, to Mama Bear, to the hunter, to the whole world.

The strange thing is that I've stopped being afraid.

I've gone right through fear and out the other side. All those millions of atoms of fear in my body have condensed into a tiny black hole of terror, about the size of an acorn, and buried themselves deep inside my stomach.

The world holds its breath. It seems like a lifetime since I flew over Snowball's neck, and yet the hunter is still frozen on the ground. His face is a Halloween mask of horror.

Mama Bear is two springs away whichever way I go.

I hold my breath, and push the spray can's trigger.

A ghost-green mist shoots out over the great white bear. She stops as suddenly as Snowball.

The mist trickles to nothing.

The bear's shaking her head, huffing anxiously.

The can's empty.

She's deciding whether or not she's going to charge me again.

There's nothing I can do.

Back away!

I'm backing, I'm backing, but I'm a long way from the truck. There's nowhere to hide. The smell of the spray is drifting back towards me; I'm coughing and crying, I can taste dirt from the muddy creek running down my face.

'I'm sorry, Mama Bear!'

The hunter will shoot her – and then he might shoot me, because I've seen him hunting where there are NO HUNTING signs. Or Mama Bear might get me first anyway. The hunter is scrambling to his feet, coughing too and grabbing his gun.

Mama Bear turns and gallops past us towards the log where Hansel and Gretel are hiding. The cubs follow her into the woods, and all three disappear.

I know I'll never see them again.

If anyone had told me that I'd actually have to use my bear spray, I'd have thought I'd be too afraid to remember how.

And if they'd said that I'd have to use it on Mama Bear, I'd have said, 'No way!' I'd have known I'd feel too bad to even try, because the three bears are part of the whole story of coming down the mountain.

In fact they're so much part of my life that I'd have laughed if anyone had told me that I'd save someone trying to shoot the cubs.

Thinking about it is different from being here. What I cared most about was me: I didn't want to be shot by a hunter or mauled by a bear. But no matter how much I hated the hunter, I didn't want to see Mama Bear attack him.

The hunter thumps to the ground as if someone's pulled his chair away. 'You're crazy, kid! You're absolutely nuts!'

He's probably right, but I don't have time to think about it. That acorn of fear in my stomach has just exploded. My nubbly oats and chocolate-chip biscuit breakfast explodes with it. It's splattering and disgusting, and it doesn't quite miss my jeans.

'Raven!'

The voice sounds exactly like my mum.

22

MAYBE LUNCHTIME, SUNDAY

There's a silver 4WD parked at the edge of the clearing and Mum is charging over the grass towards me. I don't have to see her face to know it's her.

I never knew she could run so fast.

'What are you doing with my daughter?' she screams.

I never knew she could sound so scary.

'Put that gun down and let the kid go!' shouts a man behind her.

My dad! My real dad's come to rescue me like I always knew he would!

He's tall and fit, with straight black hair and dark eyes, and he'd be good looking except right now he looks nearly as mad as Mum. He's exactly how I've always wanted my dad to look. Or one of the ways I've always wanted my dad to look.

He's not my dad.

Knowing floods through me like a creek bursting free of a dam: my dad, my real runaway dad, is not a crocodile hunter or any sort of hero. He's a skinny red-haired man who works in a computer store in Australia and goes to the beach with his new family, just like he said in the only Christmas card he ever sent me. Maybe I'll get to meet him one day, but if he didn't care enough to see me when I was born, he's not going to magically turn up just because I need him now.

It's my mum who's come to find me.

The hunter lets go of his gun, and puts his hands in the air to prove it.

Mum and I run to each other. We hang on in the tightest, safest sort of hug, that maybe you can only do when you've thought you might never see each other again, and Mum's crying as hard as me.

'Lily and Scott!' I sob, and Mum says at the same time: 'What's happened?'

I tell her as fast as I can. '. . . We've got to rescue them!'

Behind us the man who came with Mum is still shouting at the hunter, 'What's going on? What were you doing with my horse?'

'Are you people crazy?' the hunter shouts back. 'I came in by helicopter – why would I need a horse?

And I wouldn't do anything to this kid. I don't know where the heck she came from, but she saved my life.'

'I thought that was the rescue helicopter!' I exclaim.

'It's going to be,' Mum says, glaring at the hunter. 'You're going to call it in to find my daughter and husband while we wait for Search and Rescue.'

'Mobile phones don't work here,' I tell her.

'You can't tell me they dropped you off with no way of contacting them!' Mum shouts at the hunter. 'I don't care if it's a satellite phone or a walkie talkie or semaphore! Call that helicopter!'

The hunter's already pulled out what looks like a heavy, old-fashioned mobile phone and is speaking into it. 'We've got an emergency!'

The voice crackles out loud. 'Are you injured?'

'Not me. A man and a girl.'

There's a lot more crackling, and a few odd words, '. . . risky . . . fines . . . lose the chopper . . .' as if the pilot's talking to someone else.

'Just get down here!' the hunter shouts.

More crackling. 'Forget it. Call Search and Rescue, that's what they're there for.'

Before the hunter can argue again, there's a drum of horse's hooves, and Snowball gallops past the 4WD.

A woman leaps off his back and starts rubbing my

shoulder as if she wants to hug me, except I'm still snuggled into Mum and too stinky for anyone who isn't my mother to hug.

'Am I glad to see you!' she exclaims. 'Thank heavens your mum was so determined to get up here and find you! I've phoned Search and Rescue, but it could be a few hours before they get here.'

Mum reaches over and grabs the phone out of the hunter's hands.

'My husband and daughter's lives are at stake and you're worrying about *fines*? I'll pay whatever you want, but *please*, come down and help us.'

There's no answer.

'I'm sorry,' the hunter says to Mum. His eyes are slitty black with rage.

'He could lose the helicopter if he's caught using it for poaching,' Snowball's owner says.

'That's no excuse!' the hunter snaps. 'Is there any other way up the mountain?'

'This is it,' Snowball's owner says.

'So we go up on foot,' says the hunter. 'If they need digging out, Search and Rescue can do with some help. We can't just sit here!'

My knees hear the word 'sit' and I land on the ground. So does the last of my breakfast.

I open my eyes to a circle of worried faces.

Snowball's owner is handing me a bottle of sports drink.

Mum's propping me up so I can drink it, and wiping my face with a tissue from her pocket. Her face is so white and twisted that it looks as if she's in pain too.

'Raven, dearest . . . I need to go with the men. Could you stay with Amy till I get back? I met Amy and Greg at the café last night – Greg is Scott's friend from high school. When I told them I was getting worried, they offered to bring me up here first thing this morning.'

'Do you want me to take her down to the hospital for a check-up?' Amy asks. 'She's a bit of a mess.'

'It's just mud . . . and I got jiggled up from riding.' I glance up, but she doesn't seem angry about my borrowing their horse.

Mum's looking around on the ground. 'Where are your glasses?'

'I lost them when I fell off the mountain.'

'What do you mean, 'Fell off the mountain?' Mum demands.

The hunter interrupts her to hand me a fruit-and-nut bar. 'You're probably hungry. Chasing that bear took some energy.'

'Chasing *what* bear?' the others all say at once.

'Honey,' says Amy, 'let your mum go find your sister.

Sounds like you've had enough adventures for one day.'

The men put the rifle in the 4WD and come back with a crowbar and a girl's jacket that Amy puts on me, poking my arms through the sleeves as if I'm two years old. Mum still looks like she's being torn in half.

I sip my drink and nibble at the bar, and I'm being torn in half too, because I need to show them the way but I can't walk up that mountain again today.

'I marked the trail . . .' I start to say, when my voice is drowned out by a familiar noise.

The poachers' helicopter is hovering above us.

A man in a hunter's jacket jumps out the instant the helicopter runners touch the grass. He looks like a dog whose bone has been stolen, and I'm glad he's not carrying his gun.

'We can't take you all!' he snaps.

'The little girl and I are staying,' Amy says.

'No, I've got to go!'

Mum is stroking my face and smoothing my hair; she doesn't even mind her hands turning black with my mud. 'My brave girl,' she murmurs. 'You've done enough.'

'I've got to show you where they are!'

'Make up your minds!' the dog-faced man snarls.

'Are you sure?' Mum asks me.

I nod, and we hold hands to run under the whirring blades.

'The little girl better sit in the copilot's seat to show you where to go,' my hunter tells the pilot. I think he also doesn't want me to see the stag's head on the tarpaulin at the back.

Too late.

I wonder if it was the teenage deer's father.

If I throw up again Mum will make me get off and go to the hospital. I gulp down the sour sick.

The pilot helps me do up my seatbelt and put on the earmuffs. There's a singing-star microphone so I can talk to him.

Even Amelia's never been in a helicopter.

The blades whirr into a bluey blur above me, the pilot fiddles with dials and levers, and we lift gently above the clearing. The lake shimmers turquoise below my feet, stretching farther than I'd guessed between the mountains. I can see every direction, up and down and as far as I can turn my head.

'Where to, kid?'

'Nearly to the top.'

The ground below me changes; the lake and the clearing disappear and we're looking down at treetops. The forest is such a thick mass I can't see through it.

I hope the dog-faced hunter can't see through it either. I hope the bears stay in the middle of it.

I don't start shaking till we fly over the tree line.

As the helicopter lowers, I can see the scars of the new cliff I fell down, the rubble of the cemetery field, and the three great nose boulders covering Lily and Scott's cave.

It's nearly two days since I slid down from their ledge, and in a minute I'll find out if my sister and stepdad are alive or dead.

23

EARLY SUNDAY AFTERNOON

There's no sign of life.

The ledge is too narrow for the helicopter; we land at the bottom of the cliff, in the cemetery field. Mum, the hunter and Greg jump out while the blades are still whirring. The dog-faced hunter stays inside to pass them the crowbar, pick axe, ropes and blankets they'd brought from the 4WD, and hands me out like another parcel.

The door slams behind me; the engine whines louder, and the blades blur the helicopter above the rocks. It hovers over us for a minute and disappears out of sight.

'Sorry,' says the hunter.

'What matters is he got us up the mountain,' says Greg, pulling a rope out of the bundle.

'Let's get moving,' says Mum. 'Raven, you'd better stay down here.'

I don't answer. The only thing worse than climbing back up those rocks would be staying alone at the bottom.

Maybe it's the sports drink and health bar kicking in, or maybe it's because Mum's at the bottom watching – or maybe it's just that I've got a rope tied around my middle with a big man holding the other end at the top of the cliff, but going up these rocks isn't half as hard as going down.

But I'm so terrified watching Mum climb that I can hardly breathe. If something happens to her that'll be my fault too; I imagine her tumbling backwards onto the rocks . . .

'Don't worry, I'm not going to let your mum fall,' says Greg. 'I sure don't want a bear-chasing girl angry at me!'

I try to smile, but the only thing I care about is Mum scrambling onto the ledge, breathing deeply, and hugging me for no reason.

The bundle of tools and blankets, and finally the hunter, follow us up. We edge around the bend to the pile of rubble that I'd started trying to clear. It's just as high as when I left.

'Lily!' Mum screams.

Hearing Mum scream is a thousand times worse than screaming myself, and seeing the men look at each other the way they just did is a million times worse than feeling hopeless myself.

'We've got to go around to the other end,' I tell them. 'She'll hear us from there.'

The men start getting the rope ready and Greg explains that one of them should climb across first, so that Mum and I are safe in the middle again. By the time he finishes, Mum and I are half way across the first boulder.

'If you slide down here,' I tell her, 'you can step across to the next one.'

She doesn't need to be told. She's scrambling across that rock like a Mt Everest sherpa, straight across and up to the ridge. Still on her hands and knees, she reaches down and pulls me up beside her.

There's a window in the rock, and a white face peering out.

'Raven!' screams Lily. 'Mum!'

And from further back in the cave comes Scott's deep voice: 'Jenny!'

The icy lump in my heart melts and floods over me, washing me away just about to nothing. I'm not a superhero; I'm not Jess or Amelia; I'm just Raven, a skinny red-haired girl on top of a mountain. But I'm not alone anymore.

Mum and I huddle together in a blanket watching Greg and the hunter balance on the cliff above the door rock. The men had insisted that only two of them could use a crowbar at a time, and there wasn't enough room for Mum.

They jam the crowbar into the crack between the rock and the cliff.

'Ready?' the hunter shouts.

'We're clear!' Scott shouts back, from inside the cave.

'One, two, THREE!' Greg counts, and the two men push together on the crowbar.

Their faces glow red; sweat pours down their cheeks. Nothing else happens.

'Break!' pants the hunter, pulling the crowbar out. They stand up, still panting; take off their jackets and gulp from water bottles.

Greg moves a half step to the right. 'Try from here.'

The hunter nods and slides the crowbar in again.

They grit their teeth, their eyes pop; the muscles in their arms bulge and strain. Mum is rubbing my back so hard it hurts.

The rock shifts forward . . . and back again as if it's changed its mind.

'They can't hold that much longer!' says Mum.

She grabs the pick from the bundle and scrambles up beside the men. Somehow there is room for all of them.

Mum slips the pick into the new crack. It just fits.

The men pull the crowbar out and bend double, gasping and panting with their hands on their knees. Mum's arms are trembling, but she holds the pick steady.

'Ready?' says Greg, and the hunter nods. They slide the crowbar in beside the pick and heave again. Mum pushes down on her pick; the men grunt as they strain against the crowbar . . .

. . . the door rock creaks, and smashes down, over the edge of cliff.

The cave is open.

Mum slides down to the mouth of the cave as Lily staggers out, wobbly and crying. They cling to each other just the way Mum and I did at the bottom of the mountain; then I take over the hug and Mum crawls into the cave to Scott.

That's when the Search and Rescue helicopter arrives.

They bring Scott out on a stretcher. His face is white and his right leg is twisted in a way legs are never supposed to be.

My heart twists too, as if a splinter of ice is still in there after all.

Mum's holding Scott's hand, but he reaches for me with the other. 'Raven, thank God! I was afraid we'd never see you again!'

'I'm sorry.'

'Sorry?' he repeats, hugging my face against his shoulder: blood, mud, snot and all. 'I'm sorry I didn't manage to look after you! I'm so proud of you, Raven.'

The paramedic finishes putting a blow-up splint around Scott's leg. 'The helicopter can't fit everyone in with the stretcher,' he says. 'So we'll take you to the hospital first, then come back for the others.'

'I'm more worried about Raven,' says Scott. 'And Lily needs to be checked too.'

'We'll take the little girl in the first trip,' the paramedic agrees. 'She doesn't look too good.'

'I'm okay: it's just mud!'

The paramedic laughs. 'You're your father's daughter all right!'

Scott winks at me. 'That's the nicest thing anyone's ever said to me,' he says, and that last splinter of ice melts right out of my heart.

So Mum goes with Scott, and Lily and I stay with the men. The thing is that I wasn't trying to be brave – I just couldn't have gone in that helicopter without my sister. It was purely impossible.

We wait at the start of the cemetery field, wrapped in blankets and nibbling energy bars. Lily is looking around with thirsty eyes, drinking in everything she can see.

'Look at those rocks! It looks like there's a deformed Inukshuk on top of them.'

I can't see it, but I can guess.

'It was in case I couldn't show rescuers the way.'

Lily blushes. 'Sorry.'

'It *is* kind of deformed.'

'No! It's cool. I just didn't think you'd made it – it's hard to believe my little sister did all this on her own.'

I stay huddled in my blanket as Lily picks her way through the field to my poor little Inukshuk, and carries his head back to me. I can't believe she wants to keep it.

The two men are wandering around the other end of the field. 'Okay there, girls?' the hunter calls. 'Greg and I aren't far away if you need us!'

Funny how the hunter turned out to be all right: nearly as funny as Snowball's owner turning out to be Scott's old buddy Greg. I hadn't really paid attention to that when Mum told me.

'We're brothers, Scott and me!' Greg explained, wiping his eyes as the helicopter took off. 'Except for the bit about having the same mother and father.'

Greg said that the big rockfall that made the wall down by the lake changed the resort people's mind about buying the land next to the National Park, so Greg's family still owns it. He and Amy live in Jenkins Creek but come up most weekends. They have two daughters in between Lily's and my ages, which is why there was a girl's jacket in the 4WD.

'Not that we have to be friends with them,' Lily says. 'But . . .

'. . . we'll kind of know someone.'

She laughs. 'You've got hay in your hair – and a feather.'

I'd forgotten about the feather. It seems kind of silly now I'm with people again.

But Lily's not really laughing, or not much. 'It's like that raven really was looking out for you.' She pulls her comb out of her backpack, and, very gently, undoes my braid. As she starts combing out the hay and tangles, I'm thinking Jess would say she felt like Rapunzel turning back into a princess after she was lost in the forest, but I feel like me being looked after by my sister, which is a whole lot better.

'I thought maybe I wouldn't ever see you again,' Lily says.

'Me too.'

'I thought you might get lost and die, or we'd die before you got help, or both.'

'Me too. But I had to keep on going, because if you died it would be my fault.'

'You really chased a bear?'

I shiver: facing the charging Mama Bear is something I'll never forget, and I reckon that when I'm a hundred and twenty, it'll still make me shiver. 'It's not like I meant to.'

'And you stole a horse?'

'Borrowed.'

'That's so cool. Maybe we should ask Mum again about a horse, since it helped save all our lives and all.'

'Or she might never let us out of the house again.'

'If our new house didn't have so many windows I mightn't go in at all. I'm never going somewhere with no windows again.'

So that's what's going to make Lily shiver when she's a hundred and twenty-three: being closed in.

'You know the first thing I thought when I hammered out that chunk of rock and saw the full moon? It was the most beautiful thing I'd ever seen – and I thought if you were still on the mountain you'd be looking at it too.'

I want to lie and say I'd gazed up and thought about her too, but it doesn't seem like the time for fibs, even white ones. 'That was really the first thing you thought?'

'Well, after "Fresh air – I can breathe!" And "Damn! It's not big enough to get through!" It was the first thing I thought when I just calmed down and looked out.'

'I couldn't think about you too much,' I explain. 'When I thought about you and Scott in the cave, and that it might be my fault . . . it made me cry so I couldn't think.'

'I told Scott what you said, that you thought you'd started the rockfall.'

I try to swallow. 'What did he say?'

'He said maybe, if the nose had a crack that was ready to go, because it only needs a little rock to knock off a bigger one, then the bigger rock knocks off bigger ones . . .'

The biggest rock of all settles firmly in my stomach. *'Don't be silly,'* Scott's supposed to say, *just like Lily had two days ago, but nicer. 'Of course it's not your fault!'*

'He said that wasn't what mattered. It was an accident and it's what you did next that mattered.'

I remember the voice in my head saying, *If you did that, you can do anything!*

'Scott and I started talking about the worst things we've ever done. Mine was telling you our real dad left because of you.'

I can't breathe. It's not fair to talk about that today.

'It's a lie: he left because of me; because I wouldn't stop crying. You know what gets me? The one single thing I can remember about our father is him shouting at me to stop crying, and how afraid I was when he shoved me into my room and slammed the door.'

The garbage of guilt tumbles away . . . until I look at Lily and start to feel sad and angry and wise all at once. Even though I've always believed it was my fault our dad had left, just because I was born, I know for absolutely sure that it couldn't be a three-year-old's fault.

'You think a little kid could make a grown-up do something he didn't want to? You can't get Mum to do what you want now!'

Lily gives a funny sort of laugh, and we sit a while longer, shoulders rubbing, looking down at the mountain we've climbed. Far below us, we can hear the rescue helicopter on its way back to take us to Mum and Scott.

Then Lily starts braiding my hair again, dancing the strands from side to middle to the other side, each one taking turns, but with the raven's feather always firm and unmoving at the centre.

24

Flying down the mountain with my sister, the peak still looks fierce and bare; the chain of mountains around it are still endless and empty. I've got the binoculars from Scott's pack, so I can see it all now too.

We hover over the raggedy tree line, the berry field and the secret cave waterfall; I show Lily the little waterfalls cascading to the Niagara, pretty and sparkling in the sun as if they'd never tried to drown me. Off to the right we can see the creek that I followed to the marsh, and the gentler hills of Greg's ranch.

I don't exactly know what I feel about the mountain, except that I want Lily not to hate it.

'Look at that!' the pilot says through the headsets as we hover above the riverbank. 'I've never seen a white bear out here before!'

Mama Bear stands guard to watch the helicopter go by. The pilot doesn't see the cubs, nestled together in the long grass, and I keep their secret. They're wild and free, and safe.

Lily smiles, and squeezes my hand.

ABOUT THE AUTHOR

Wendy Orr was born in Edmonton, Canada, and spent her childhood in various places across Canada, France, and the USA, but wherever she lived, there were lots of stories, adventures and animals. Wendy fell in love with the mountains when was eight and went to summer camp in the Rockies. When she was twelve, she climbed Pike's Peak in Colorado with her father and sister, and will never forget the thrill of reaching the top!

Raven's Mountain is set in the high mountain country of British Columbia in Canada. This area is the home of many wild animals, including grizzlies and black bears. And very occasionally, a rare white Spirit Bear from the central coast of British Columbia has also been spotted further inland . . .

Wendy is the author of several award-winning books,

including *Nim's Island, Nim at Sea, Spook's Shack, Mokie and Bik*, and for teenagers, *Peeling the Onion*.

A few years after Wendy wrote *Nim's Island*, a film producer in Hollywood took the book out of the library to read to her son, and the next day emailed Wendy to ask if she could make it into a movie. Wendy said yes! They became good friends and Wendy had the fun of helping work on the screenplay, and learning that making a movie was even more complicated than writing a book.

Wendy Orr lives on Victoria's Mornington Peninsula with her dog and other family.

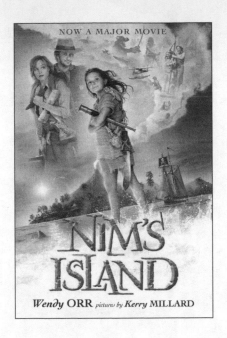

NIM'S ISLAND

Nim lives on an island in the middle of the wide blue sea
with her father Jack, a marine iguana called Fred, a sea lion
called Selkie, a turtle called Chica and a satellite dish
for her email. No one else in the world lives quite like Nim,
and she wouldn't swap places with anyone.

But when Jack disappears in his sailing boat, and disaster
threatens her home, Nim must be braver than she's ever been
before. And she needs help from her friends, old and new.

Nim's Island is also a movie, starring Abigail Breslin,
Jodie Foster and Gerard Butler.

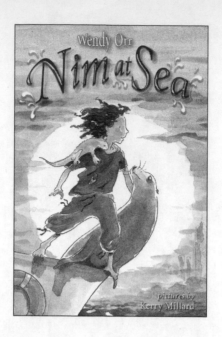

NIM AT SEA

Nim lives on an island in the middle of the wide blue sea
with her father Jack, a marine iguana called Fred, a sea lion
called Selkie, and their new friend Alex Rover. Nim is as free
as a bird, and she wouldn't swap places with anyone.

But when Alex flies away in the seaplane, without saying
goodbye, and Selkie is captured by villains from a cruise ship,
Nim must risk everything to bring them back. Her dangerous
rescue mission takes her far across the ocean, to New York
City. It's a good thing she has Fred and two new friends
by her side.